MAKING
OF A
POLICE
STATE

THE SOCIALIST AGENDA
FOR
AMERICA

BY
STEVE LAWRENCE

Order this book online at www.trafford.com
or email orders@trafford.com

Most Trafford titles are also available at major online book retailers.

Print information available on the last page.

ISBN: 978-1-4120-6837-6 (sc)
ISBN: 978-1-4122-3873-1 (e)

Trafford rev. 04/16/2020

 www.trafford.com
North America & international
toll-free: 1 888 232 4444 (USA & Canada)
fax: 812 355 4082

Steve Lawrence is a typical American who served honorably for 22 years in the U.S. Military. A second generation American, his love for America is overwhelming. Married for over 30 years with five children he is concerned the freedom he grew up with and defended may not exist for his 4 grandchildren. He has not only studied governments and societies but lived them first hand. Throughout his military career he lived in 6 different countries in Europe, Asia, the South Pacific and the Middle East and experienced extended temporary tours in a dozen other countries in Africa, Central and South America. The majority of the time he lived in the communities of the host country which afforded him opportunities the majority of Americans will never experience or even understand. After developing severe health problems due to his military service he and his family wished to retire to a small farm to be left alone. This did not happen. After repeated domestic assaults on the US Constitution and usurpation of power by local politicians he decided to take the most effective course of action left to him. Steve dedicated much of his life in defending the freedoms Americans enjoy and now through his writings continue to bring the assaults on these freedoms to light in hope of continuing this defense.

This book is dedicated to my grandparents for having the courage to step into an unknown future and legally immigrate to America, and to my Father, the oldest of the first generation of our family in America and a member of the last great generation of America to fight for our rights and freedoms against fascism and tyranny in World War II.

"...The most important words in the Constitution are the ones that begin with: "We the people..." This idea of government is beholden to the people, that it has no other source of power except the sovereign people, is still the newest and most unique idea in all the long history of man's relation to man... whether we believe in our capacity for self-government or whether we abandon the American Revolution and confess that a little intellectual elite in a far-distant capital can plan our lives for us better than we can plan them ourselves. You and I are told increasingly that we have to choose between left or right. There is only an up or down: up to man's age-old dream-the ultimate in individual freedom consistent with law and order-or down to the ant heap of totalitarianism. And regardless of their sincerity, their humanitarian motives, those who would trade our freedom for security have embarked on this downward course." — Ronald Reagan vi

CONTENTS

CHAPTER ONE

The Socialist are Coming!
The Socialist are Coming!

Much like Paul Revere warning "The British are coming", initiating a call to arms, this is a call to action. All freedom loving Americans should be vigilant for attacks on our country as well as our freedoms from domestic as well as foreign origins. Although slightly different, the oath of office/service for military personnel as well as elected officials generally states:

> "I, (name), do solemnly swear (or affirm) that I will support and defend the Constitution of the United States against all enemies, foreign and domestic; that I will bear true faith and allegiance to the same; that I take this obligation freely, without any mental reservation or purpose of evasion; and that I will well and faithfully discharge the duties of the office on which I am about to enter. So help me God."

Unfortunately, many of our elected representatives and judges are not living up to this oath. There are many domestic attacks against the U.S. Constitution by these members of the legislature as well as judicial branches of government with an occasional attack by the executive branch. The majority of these attacks go unnoticed because we the people expect to trust these elected and appointed representatives. Anytime you hear of any law infringing on any individual right especially those reaffirmed and protected under the Bill of Rights is an attack on the US Constitution.

The Founding Fathers were visionaries when they penned the constitution by including the phrase "…**enemies, foreign and domestic**" because they knew it would only be a matter of time before some elected officials would attempt to dismantle the US Constitution through devious and subversive ways. You should read the Federalist Papers to get an insight in the minds of the Founding Fathers about this.

Some of these representatives attacking the Constitution feel they are doing the right thing; some are intimidated by others, while many don't respect the oath of office and wish to push the socialist agenda. These are the ones who erroneously think they know what's best for the people and hold themselves as the "enlightened" few. The following quote is very relevant and sums up a major symptom of these people! "The first sign of corruption in a society that is still alive is that the end justifies the means." Georges Bernanos (1888 - 1948)

You know the ones. These elitists routinely preach to do what they say, and omit, not what they do. Many feel the freedom of speech pertains to them and those who support their causes, right to bear arms apply to only the elitists and not the "common" people, social security isn't good enough for them so they have their own retirement system and on and on. When you move to the elitists at the county and municipal levels and ones who do not hold public office it gets even worse.

Many are asking what is going on in America at this moment. We appear to have lost the direction of the Founding Fathers. One has to look no farther than the current state of affairs to know what the problem is and who or what is behind the "decay" of our great country. Although many reasons can be attributed to this, the socialist/collective mentality which permeates our society is primarily to blame.

Don't confuse liberalism with socialism/elitist. The "extreme left" are the true socialists and has hijacked the term "liberal" from the moderate left.

3

You'll find most liberals and conservatives are more centrist. The majority of Americans are centrist as most share some liberal views as well as conservative and many consider themselves independent.

Those who have only liberal or only conservative beliefs are far left or right. Then you have the extremists of the left and right. The extremists on the right are usually kept in check by the more moderate and their radicalism is more evident. For the most part the extreme right doesn't have the media complicity enjoyed by the extreme left. The extremists of the left are far more deceitful and conniving as evidenced by their hijacking of the liberal label. Many high profile politicians exhibit this extremist behavior as apparent in their rhetoric, voting records and other items they support. They promote the give-a-way philosophy and feel the government should be responsible for everyone's welfare.

Many of these far left politicians are taking the advice of some very public strategists/advisors and delivering speeches indicating they are moving to the center. According to at least one democratic strategist's suggestion of essentially deceiving the electorate and then performing as always once elected. Politicians like Hillary Clinton's voting record and behavior in my opinion indicates she is far left but her speeches since the 2004 elections has her moving toward the center*. Her senate voting and actions indicates she is not moving to the center. The ones who appear to be extremists of the left, such as, Ted Kennedy, John Kerry, Nancy Pelosi and the many others, make Hillary Clinton more appealing to a more centrist electorate. We'll discuss this type of deception in depth a little later.

What is the socialist agenda? Are the liberals really behind it? How about the American Civil Liberties Union (ACLU)? What about the United Nations (U.N.)? Would you believe the American Association of Retired People (AARP)? It would be difficult to say any one entity is behind it as it is more of a mindset. Many different organizations are only the vessels to deliver this failed mentality and push this agenda. It would seem one of the key objectives would be to remove individual responsibility for ones actions and place the blame on society. Unless, of course, you are either a conservative or moderate and then you must be attacked and/or controlled.

The mindset has existed long before the U.N. and modern elitists. It seems to fester within the ranks of the "educated". The so called intellectually elite in the third world countries as well as the industrialized self righteous who believe the United States should care

5

for the world's needy and the "state" knows best for all and individualism is bad. These elitists feel the United States is the cause of the world's problems. The fact of the matter is the United States provides aid, both monetary and humanitarian, more than any other country in the world. The real problem is no matter what we do for the needy, it will never be enough in the eye of these socialist. Their ideal is known as utopian socialism with a twist. Most of us work, many of them don't.

Many countries throughout the world have been moving in this direction for decades. This socialist movement can easily be seen in many European countries as well as many in the rest of the world*. In Italy you can receive a pension after working for only five years. The United States has been the great holdout mainly because we hold our freedom so dearly and our government is supposed to be dictated by the people.

You may ask, "How can this equate to a police state for America?" Simple, in order for their concept to work, American citizens have to be controlled. This book will explore things we see in our everyday lives that exposes the socialist trends and attempts to control you. What the socialist can't control, they attempt to destroy.

ACLU — American Civil Liberties Union.

"The price of freedom is eternal vigilance." Thomas Jefferson. This statement is as pertinent today as it was over two hundred years ago. If we fail to recognize the internal threat, the United States will no longer exist as a free nation of individuals, but, as a nation existing for the "collective" interests of the few elitists.

Religious freedom is under attack by the elitist as well. The socialist can talk hate about your religious belief but look at what can happen when the shoe is on the other foot. Does your 501 (c) 3 incorporated church's preach anything "contrary to clearly defined public policy" (IRS pub 557 pg 20) such as preaching against abortion or sodomy? If it does, your pastor can now be hauled out of the pulpit and locked up until he has posted bond…, (if and when the judge decides to set a bond amount) Are provisions supporting this in the United States Constitution? Of course not! Though the ACLU would have you believe it does. However, it does exist in the Former Soviet Union Constitution*;

"Article 52 [Religion]
(1) Citizens of the USSR are guaranteed freedom of conscience, that is, the right to profess or not to profess any religion, and to conduct religious worship or atheistic propaganda. Incitement of hostility or hatred on

religious grounds is prohibited..." (Emphasis mine)

We'll discuss incidents with law enforcement, schools and education, private ownership of property, bureaucrats within all levels of the United States and local government and many other issues we have become desensitized to. Desensitization is one of the most useful tools along with indoctrination of our youth to achieve the socialist goal. For well over forty years the American people have been manipulated by the elitist who have attempted to shape our minds and infiltrate our society throughout the government, media and education system. Many are unwitting participants who have been deceived into believing things that are not true and many times undermine the very freedoms we hold dear.

The elitists are scattered all around. The prominent ones can be seen or heard about in the media. You have the anti-gun crowd such as Rosie O'Donald*, Diane Feinstein*, Michael Moore* to name a few. You know Ms. O'Donald as the one who verbally attacked Tom Selleck for promoting firearms and making movies using firearms on her television show. What was Ms. O'Donald's response when her bodyguard applied for a concealed weapons permit in Connecticut? How about Michael Moore, who infamously produced a propagandist film distorting firearms ownership in America and touting "America as a culture of fear", when his bodyguard was busted for illegal handgun possession in the JFK airport in New York? The most blatant is anti-rights Senator Dianne Feinstein when receiving a CCW in California. She stated she was threatened and felt she needed protection. She's a US Senator and has security or law enforcement whenever she walks down the street. She should be a single mother in Washington D.C. with a crack-head or violent ex-husband/boyfriend in a high crime neighborhood if she really wants to see what threatened feels like. In many states only the wealthy or influential can afford a permit. The elitists such as Ted Kennedy want to place an exorbitant tax on ammo in order to control the average person. This tax may result in a box of ammo costing well over a hundred dollars. Only the elitist can afford something like this.

Remember, these elitists think the rules apply to you, not them. This personal example reflects how many of these elitists think the rules don't apply to them. Shortly after retiring from the U.S. Military my family and I returned home to live on a small farm. I had a fairly late model pickup, which for many city dwellers, denote redneck. I had to go to the store to get some supplies and groceries. One of my sons was with me as we pulled into the parking lot. I turned into a one way parking row where the cars were diagonally parked.

It was obvious this was a one way as the direction of the cars parked and the arrows on the road surface. As soon as I turned I stopped for someone who was just getting into their car to leave. I had about 3 feet of space between my truck and both sides of the curb. Before the gentleman could back out a Ford Expedition swung around cutting through the parking spaces and heading up the wrong way. The woman driving squeezed between my truck and the parked cars stopping only because the curb was in her way. Her angle blocked the gentleman who was attempting to leave.

Then a middle aged woman was driving a Mercedes full of teenagers cut across the parking spaces and pulled behind the SUV. The woman driving the SUV started blowing her horn. Since her position put her window right next to my mine I rolled my window down. She refused to look at me but her passenger looked at me and I guess the angry look I had scared her as she motioned for her friend to take off. She jumped the curb in her SUV and took off.

The lady in the Mercedes pulled up beside me and began honking her horn. After a minute she rolled her window down and looked at me with a very disapproving expression. She told me I was blocking her in and I needed to move. I told her she was going the wrong way and had no right to subject those kids to a blatant violation of traffic laws. She became indignant and said "I'm driving a Mercedes and I have a right to drive any way I want". I told her she was wrong and I was not moving and she could use her cell phone to call the police and then we would see who would get a ticket. With that she backed up and went around and parked somewhere else.

This is typical of the elitist. These two looked down on me because I was driving a pickup and they had their luxury vehicles therefore I had to be some uneducated redneck who should bow to their aristocracy.

It doesn't stop there. The best example is while I was on terminal leave waiting for my retirement from the military. One of my sons was in junior high and had a career day. Since we had spent most of our time overseas and they attended Department of Defense schools and this school was a regular school, this was something new and special. He asked if I would wear my uniform and give a presentation of what my job in the military was like. His vice principal called and asked and thought it would be great for a military person to speak to the children. I agreed and called the local recruiter to arrange permission for wear of the uniform and guidelines.

The fateful day came and I dressed in "blues" without the coat but with full ribbon display. I was greeted by the vice principal and taken to the library with the rest of the parent/presenters. We were told we would be there most of the day and would give our presentations from 4 to 6 times in separate classrooms. There were about a dozen 12 foot long tables in the library and I sat at the end of one.

More presenters entered and sat at other tables. Everyone entering appeared to make a conscious effort to sit at the other tables. When the seats at those tables were filled newcomers would stand rather than sit at the table I was sitting at. Some of these were doctors, lawyers, local politicians, corporate business owners and other type of professionals. Although I attempted to talk with some of them, none would remain in proximity well enough for a conversation. They were all talking in their small groups and I managed to overhear much of their conversations.

The most appalling was the conversation between a lawyer and a city councilman. They were talking about how stupid and uneducated the electorate was and their only salvation was the politicians and lawyers. I could take it no more when I left my seat and tactfully entered the conversation. I engaged both of them in constitutional law and cited several laws in violation of the constitution. This is the first time I heard some idiot say the constitution is a "living document". I challenged this statement citing specific references in the constitution as well as notes from Jefferson, Washington, Adams and others. Thomas Jefferson's quote, "An honest man can feel no pleasure in the exercise of power over his fellow citizens", took them by surprise. I asked if either had read the Federalist Papers! Neither had and the councilman didn't even know what they were. I told them if they were not familiar with these writings their argument is not based on fact but emotion and opinion.

They asked what my education was and I told them not to confuse education with intelligence. I asked what their IQs were. The lawyer said his was around 130 while the councilman said his was about 118. They wanted to know what mine was. I had only completed an in-depth IQ evaluation a year before and was just under 160. This intrigued them as why would someone with an IQ like this serve a career in the military. I asked, "Do you enjoy your jobs, houses, families and freedoms?" They both replied yes. I told them there is no higher purpose in this country than to protect freedom and the opportunity to succeed such as what has been given to them. I don't know if it changed their minds but at least I tried.

Anyway, we separated and gave our presentations. Many of the kids in the first class were obviously from elitists households. Only one teacher was present and was very nice. I gave a brief description of basic training and technical training everyone had to attend before performing their primary specialty. I gave them in-depth information of what a career in the military was like for me. I told them of the difficulties and challenges of living in several different countries for almost ten years. How three of my five children were born and raised in foreign countries. I gave a brief session on the Persian Gulf War and the aftermath as well as being deployed aboard a ship with over 200 US Marines for several months during the Haitian Boatlift of 1994. The kids asked a ton of pertinent questions of which I answered. I felt as though I had given them a whole new understanding of the military.

The second class I talked with seemed to be more excited. There were also three teachers in this session. I essentially gave the same presentation and answered questions from students and teachers alike. The teachers who appeared to be standoffish at first were starting to warm and took a real interest in what I was saying. By the last session I had as many teachers as students. What surprised me the most was the lawyer I had talked with earlier was there along with a couple of other parents/presenters and they seemed more interested than the students.

After it was all over with several of the parents came up to me and said I had opened their eyes to things they never knew. They seemed appreciative and thankful. I feel as though I had entered the heart of the elitist den and managed to come away victorious in the fact I may have changed some minds to have a better understanding of what America is all about. A country of the people!

CHAPTER TWO

The Socialist Mantra

How many times have you heard, "For the children…", "For public safety…" or "For security…" when these people assault your constitutionally protected freedoms. The people who lead these assaults know the way to get public opinion on their side is to convince you to give up some of your rights to push their agenda. As Thomas Jefferson stated "The man who would choose **security** over **freedom** deserves neither." The elitists don't understand the individual right takes priority over the collective right.

The far left extremists lead you to believe the right are behind infringing on your liberties. Open your eyes and see who is really behind usurping power to deprive you of freedom. I've heard several quiet conversations of these extremists and discovered they are almost jubilant over the Patriot Act although publicly they decry the infringements on our freedoms. Many are biding their time until they return to power so they may use the Patriot Act to strip your freedoms in the name of security. Personal ownership of firearms is high on their list as is censoring anyone who opposes them. Look across the nation at lower levels of government where the far left hold power to see what's in store for us if they manage to return to power.

Let me preface much of what I am about to discuss by saying I make my own decisions about my personal safety and security. I will also say individual actions are controlled whereas "collective" actions are rewarded. Think about some of the so-called safety issues that have been drafted into law.

Laws requiring seatbelts are some of the most troublesome and intrusive. We've heard the safety issue for seatbelts concerning personal injury. The legislatures have been lobbied by those who convinced them the people (meaning you) cannot think for themselves and should have this imposed on them. You, who work for a living, pay your bills, and/or raise a family among numerous other things demonstrating your responsibility and analytical skills are very capable of making the decision to wear or not wear a seatbelt. The government has overstepped their mandate and imposed this requirement on you. Personally I always wear a seatbelt because I believe you'd be crazy not to.

In Lago Vista, Texas in 1997, a lady* was driving her kids home from a soccer game. A toy fell out of the vehicle in their neighborhood and was retracing their route slowly so that the kids might be able to spot the lost toy. A police officer pulled her over and barked at her for not keeping her kids in their seatbelts. Instead of issuing her a ticket, the cop put her in handcuffs and took her into custody. Luckily for her family, a neighbor arrived on the scene just in time to spare the children from temporary foster care. The police officer handcuffed her with her hands behind her back, placed her in the police car, and drove to the police station. Ironically, the officer did not secure her in a seat belt for the drive. At the station, she was forced to remove her shoes, relinquish her possessions and wait in a holding cell for about an hour.

You have the right to make this basic and personal decision in the privacy of your own vehicle. These people have convinced lawmakers otherwise and you have allowed yourself to be penalized. You see, the government doesn't allow you, but, you allow the government. These socialists do not want you to understand this. This is a prime example of how personal decisions are controlled. Take the same subject concerning seatbelts and public transportation. You can get on a bus, subway, taxi, etc… and not be required to wear a seatbelt. This is an excellent example of how "collective" behavior/actions are rewarded and personal ones are penalized.

Another "for the children" is bike helmets. Although, bike helmets are a good idea, I believe it is the decision of the parents and child. A child under ten would best be advised to wear one and those over ten usually have the wherewithal to decide if they need one or not. The government has no right to require you to wear one. More children are injured and/or killed every year from falling down stairs than from bicycle accidents according to the CDC. Does that mean you should require your children to wear a protective helmet when around any stairs? As absurd as this may sound there is very little difference between the two. In some instances, well meaning people have been misled about many of the facts and push for these restrictive "safety" measures. Am I promoting not wearing safety equipment? Not in the least. I am saying it is your decision, not the governments, to use or not use this type of equipment. If you really want people to use safety equipment such as seatbelts and bike helmets there is another way.

Instead of the government infringing on your decision making convince insurance companies to add a line to their policies stating, "Failure to use proper safety equipment may result in decreased benefits in the result of injuries of this failure". Believe me, this will encourage compliance quicker than any government dictate and the decision will ultimately be the individual's, as it should be.

Another really hot topic "for public safety" and "for the children" is firearms. This is the most attacked and the most feared by the extremists. Some studies showing the danger to children are biased to the point of being laughable if this subject weren't so serious. I remember reading one study that was shelved when the desired results contradicted the desired outcome.

This study was supposed to place a number of young children in a room with handguns (unloaded and unable to fire) on the coffee table to gauge their behavior and reaction. Half of the children were from homes without firearms and the other half were from homes with firearms where the child was provided gun safety instruction. The children without firearms in the home picked up the handguns and began playing with them while the other children cautioned them and said an adult should be present for them to handle the handgun.

This outcome did not fit the agenda of this organization so the "study" was shelved and a new one was conducted. The new one had about a dozen children from homes without firearms. None of the test subjects had been exposed to firearms or safety training. Needless to say, the results for this group provided exactly what the organizers wanted. This time almost all the children handled the handguns, thrilling the people who wanted to show the dangers of firearms and children.

My personal experience, although not scientific, reflects the need for firearm safety to be taught to children at a very early age. I've always had handguns, long guns and shot guns in my home and my five children were exposed to them from the time they could walk. I did not shoot around them until they were about four years old. I did teach them safety long before then. Each of my children had been taught the destructive power of a firearm. I would squat with one of my kids between my arms and against my chest with them looking out. I then would have them wrap their little hands around the handgun with my hands over the top of theirs so I could absorb most of the repercussion. We would fire at a milk bottle full of water which would essentially explode on impact.

You could feel the repercussion from the handgun as the wind blew your hair and could feel it on your face and understand the power it exerted when fired. The target exploding was impressive and it didn't take the kids long to know firearms were not toys. After providing them this experience I would occasionally test them to ensure they understood the danger firearms posed.

I would clean my firearms and make sure they were unloaded and unable to fire. Every once in a while I would "leave" a firearm down where the children had access and discreetly monitored the situation. In each situation I did this, my children did not touch the firearm but kept the other children away from it and waited for mommy or daddy to return and immediately told them about the gun.

I didn't realize how good of a job we had done in firearms safety until one day my fourth child, who was about eight years old at the time, brought a friend into our house. I had a gun rack with a shotgun and rifle on the wall in the master bedroom that was easily seen from the hallway. I came home early from work and none of the kids knew I was home. I was in the master bath when I heard my son and his friend in the hallway heading toward his room. His friend stopped and I could hear him say "Wow, look at those guns. Let's play with them." To my utter amazement my son said, "Those are real and are not toys, they can hurt or kill you." His friend was insistent but my son was more insistent and demanded they go outside. Of all my children, he was the one I had the most fear of disregarding the safety I had instilled in him.

After this experience, I have no doubt education of children concerning firearms will save more than any restrictions ever will. Another comparison between firearms and motor vehicles sheds more light on the disparity of the failed gun control argument. The number of all firearms deaths worldwide is approximately 200,000. The United Nations and World Health Organization inflate this number to 500,000. These socialists believe if you state something often enough then everyone will believe it to be true. To clarify this, a piece called "Global Deaths from Firearms By David B. Kopel, Paul Gallant & Joanne D. Eisen"* gives detailed explanation as to the more correct lower number. These are for all firearm related deaths including murder, suicide, combat and instruments of war.

Compare the worldwide firearms death rate with the worldwide motor vehicle death rate of approximately 1.3 million cited by the WHO. Which is the greater threat to your safety? The main reason the socialists essentially want to ban your firearms is you will then be easily controlled and manipulated.

Another "public safety" issue is building a home. If you have purchased a small plot of land in the country and wish to build a house, many counties require you to submit plans for approval and then purchase permits. Why? If you are building your house yourself and have no intentions of selling anytime in the foreseeable future there should be no need for you to submit plans and buy permits. When the inspection office is asked why this is needed, the reply is for public safety to ensure the house is safe for you to live in.

What a bogus excuse in their attempt to control you. The county in which I reside didn't require permits or building inspections for private homes until 17 years ago. Using their failed logic all homes built before then would have to be condemned. When asked about this the reply is those homes are "grandfathered" and do not have to meet code requirements. Think about that! You are required to have your new home inspected as it is being built, for public safety, but these older homes are deemed safe by virtue of their age.

I had a discussion with a building inspector about the scam being perpetrated on citizens concerning the "codes" and requiring building inspections. I asked him why he thinks the current codes and inspections made any difference compared to 50 to 100 years ago. He said the code requirements made houses stronger and safer and the inspections ensured these standards were met. I told him I could prove otherwise.

Around the spring of 2000 a series of tornadoes tore through the Alabama/Mississippi border around Columbus. The job I had at the time took me to this area for a few days. I had the good fortune to survey much of the damage in the area. One noticeable area was homes built in the 1920s and 1930s surrounded with 100+ year old oak trees. Some of the trees were blown down but minimal damage was done to some of the houses and others were not even damaged. According to local residents I talked with said a tornado came right through their properties hitting houses trees and blowing some of their vehicles away before moving to the "new" houses at the end of their street.

These new houses were a recent development where the land was strip cleared and houses placed on very small lots. The first several houses located not more than a few yards from where these old, built without codes and inspection houses were. These "new" houses were gone. The only thing left was a concrete slab and debris. Of the 50 or so homes in this new, code compliant, inspected neighborhood about half were destroyed or severely damaged with the rest suffering considerable damage. The difference between the old and new houses was the old ones, although not complying with the building code, were stout and built to last.

During a discussion with one housing inspector I explained I wished to build according to the old standards when people built their own houses. He told me I could do this as long as I adhered to the "code". I told him I would use the necessary code for all electrical wiring and plumbing but exceed the code in the actual framing and general construction of the house. When I informed him I would use solid boards instead of plywood/OSB sheathing, he said that wasn't in the code. I stated I was using real board lumber as I was building a house to last several hundred years unlike these development houses projected for 75 to 100 years.

His reply boiled down to what it's really all about. They don't expect (or even want) these houses to last that long. When questioned further on this he became evasive and was suddenly late for an appointment. I don't blame him, for he is only being manipulated by the powers that be to enforce these unconstitutional requirements on an unsuspecting citizenry.

This cry for public safety spills over into your personal areas of choice throughout the country. Do you want or accept a group telling you what you can drink, eat, wear, drive and how to live? Why be told you can't smoke*? I don't smoke and definitely do not promote smoking. There are companies who are now terminating employees for smoking period. Can you imagine being told you will be fired if you eat red meat in your diet?

This comes under the guise of public safety and general welfare to promote healthy living. Once again the "I know what's best for you" crowd is attempting to dictate how you live your life. If left unchecked, where will this elitism end? What about the single person who may be promiscuous or the married person who may have a lover on the side? What about the car you drive. Imagine your company telling you the car you drive, the best you can afford with the meager wage they pay you, doesn't meet their minimum safety standards. Therefore, you either A-have to buy another car which meets their safety requirements or B-you're fired!

How about the neighborhood you live in. It may be the best you can afford and you call it home. Your boss just received the demographic comparison and you happen to live in a high crime area therefore are more likely to suffer from a violent crime, in turn causing medical treatment and/or hospitalization which causes the insurance premiums to rise.

Sound ridiculous? Then why are you sitting idle while others, although their habit may be unhealthy, are under attack by these elitists who will move on to one of your habits eventually. You can bet this will not stop at smoking. Think of the activities that could be added to this list. Scuba diving would make a nice safety issue for employees. Do you have a swimming pool in your yard? Then you must have a trained life guard present. That diving board is hazardous so it too must go. Do you enjoy riding a motorcycle? What are you going to do when your company tells you it's not acceptable anymore?

You see, this is just a small first step. You will see other "high risk" activities restricted if this first one is allowed to fall. Many of these people call themselves progressive thinkers. Be wary of anyone who claims to be a progressive, as everything I've seen coming from the progressives is from a collective point of view. Of course, their rules apply to everyone but them. If you take a close look at this so-called progressive mentality it is actually regressive. Much of what they espouse resembles the feudal system as the wealthy or intellectuals (lords) are dictating to those they deem lesser intellectually and or economically (peasants).

These elitists truly feel they know what's best for you since they are the enlightened few. The United States is under siege by the ruling elite. I predict this will become known as the "Age of Arrogance". They "feel" they have all the answers and have the right to tell everyone else how to live.

Another socialist mantra is the "disenfranchised" or minorities. The so-called disenfranchised are the modern voter base these elitists prey on. A good reflection of this could be seen in a Fox News Watch broadcast May 28, 2005. The topic was local news bias in reporting local crime and other negative events. Most of the panel was in agreement, minorities were reported more often in a bad light. One of the conservative members recalled an experience of attending a business conference in which many of the local black entrepreneurs and business owners were praised and presented awards for their accomplishments. He said there was virtually no mention of this event in the local media. He felt the local media was performing an injustice by not covering this event. A liberal member of the panel essentially said the local media usually presents minorities in a negative way and perhaps there should be a cap on crime reporting involving minorities to cut down on the negative perceptions it creates. The differences here are not the exception but the norm when it comes to liberals and conservatives. The conservative's view was to accentuate the positive while the liberal's solution was censorship.

This reminds me of a cancer quietly growing and spreading throughout the body causing small irritants but nothing that would cause alarm until something major happens. Many people ignore the small signs until big ones appear. By the time many people realize something serious is wrong it is usually too late. If one is fortunate enough to identify their cancer early enough it can be eradicated, if not, it will consume all healthy tissue. The elitists/socialists are like a cancer. This mentality is growing behind the scenes wreaking havoc on many of our lives throughout the country. Much like the cancer, this consumption is not of healthy tissue but of our freedom. If we fail to confront these attacks this cancer will result in the death of our country!

CHAPTER THREE

Desensitization
And
Indoctrination

Desensitization is one of the primary tools the socialist have in their arsenal. This tool has been used for centuries but did not have the impact as it now does due to the advent of modern communications.

The American Medical Association, the American Academy of Pediatrics, the American Psychological Association, and the American Academy of Child and Adolescent Psychiatry released comments on the correlation between violence and the media*. They concluded, from thirty years of research, that viewing entertainment violence does lead to an increase in aggressive attitudes, values, and behaviors in children. What they don't tell you is how this desensitization can be used to push other agendas.

The process goes like this. Begin exposure to issues you'd like a subject to be desensitized. Over time this desensitization leads to tolerance, which eventually will lead to acceptance. At least that's the expectation of ones who are pushing their agenda.

Remember sitcoms in the late sixties and early seventies? They were something new, different and exciting. The way for some of these sitcoms were paved a bit earlier to soften American society to be more receptive. The actors were young and aspiring and very entertaining and didn't realize what they were a part of.

Let's start with a show called "Three's Company". This comedy was about a man and two women who share an apartment. In order to be allowed to rent this apartment the man apparently pretended to be a homosexual. This was a very entertaining show and the actors were exceptional. It seemed harmless enough and we all got a good laugh out of it. In 1977, Billy Crystal played one of the first openly homosexual roles, Jodie Dallas, in the soap-opera satire "Soap". This was an explosively funny show and gained much notoriety in America. It also went a long way in softening the perceptions of homosexuals.

After these shows came other subtle appearances of homosexuals in Hollywood productions. The movie "Beverly Hills Cop" showed a now well known actor depicting a homosexual helping the star, Eddie Murphy, by giving him some fruit. Watch the movie and you'll see the scene. While it's not a homosexual scene it leaves no doubt as to the actor's demeanor and preference. A little more exposure equals a little more tolerance which is not entirely bad.

Next, we saw more expanded roles for homosexuals culminating into full blown roles in television and movies during the nineties. Now there are major movies and television shows depicting stars in major roles as homosexuals. Although it took over 20 years, you can clearly see the desensitization leading to tolerance with the end result of acceptance by society as a whole.

About the same time the homosexual desensitizing began so did cross dressing/transsexual behavior. To start with, look at Tootsie released in 1982 starring Dustin Hoffman in the lead role as Michael Dorsey, a desperate out of work actor who can't find a job. That is, until he gets a female role in a soap opera and becomes very famous. Nobody knows this new television star is a man. After a while, he falls in love with the leading actress of the series, and the big problem is how can he express his feelings, since she thinks that Michael is a woman? A very entertaining movie but has underlying theme of cross-dressing.

Another good example released the same year is Victor/Victoria starring Julie Andrews and James Garner. The movie starts as Victoria as a poverty-stricken soprano trying to find work in turn-of-the-century Paris. With the help of a worldly-wise nightclub singer (Robert Preston), her alter-ego Victor is invented. Victor is a female impersonator who is hired to sing at a fashionable night spot. "The plot is a woman pretending to be a man pretending to be a woman. Interwoven throughout the comedy and musical numbers are some surprisingly astute observations about gender perceptions, discrimination and the battle of the sexes."

These opened the door for "To Wong Foo, Thanks for Everything!" released in 1995. This movie begins with Vida Boheme (Patrick Swayze) and Noxeema Jackson (Wesley Snipes) winning a major New York drag contest and a trip to Hollywood, they are persuaded to take the inexperienced 'drag princess' Chi Chi (John Leguizamo) with them. "They acquire an old beat-up Cadillac and set off for L.A., but their car breaks down in a small town in the middle of nowhere. With just their wits and an endless supply of garish costumes, they transform the town and everyone who lives there until a homophobic Sheriff catches up with them."

One of the latest is Connie and Carla released in 2004. After these 2 singers accidentally witness a mafia hit in Chicago, gal pals Connie (Nia Vardalos) and Carla (Toni Collette) skip town and make a run for Los Angeles, where they go way undercover as singing drag queens working the city's dinner theater circuit. "They become big hits on the scene but things get extra-weird when Connie meets Jeff (David Duchovny), a guy she'd like to be a woman with."

All these movies are entertaining but you can see a clear pattern. There are more movies during the past few years which contribute to this pattern. Note beginning with "Tootsie" the main character was isolated, providing limited exposure to the viewers. Victor/Victoria threw a few more in the mix and the viewers were none the wiser. A few other movies with these themes occurred over the next few years and then "To Wong Foo, Thanks for Everything!" hit the screen taking a much more direct role in promoting transsexual behavior and causing only a small uproar at the time. Almost 10 years later "Connie and Carla" is released with an even more direct promotion of this lifestyle and barely created a ripple. These are good examples of how Hollywood has used desensitizing to promote deviant lifestyles. This manipulation is very subtle as all these movies are comedies. What better way to disarm people than to make them laugh. People are almost always more tolerant and accepting of comedy rather than drama.

Let me make it clear I am not a homophobe. I have many friends who are homosexual and they for the most part understand my views on homosexuality. As a Christian I condemn the homosexual lifestyle but not the individual. I strongly feel each person must answer for their own sins as I will answer for mine. Luke 6:37 — "Judge not, and ye shall not be judged: condemn not, and ye shall not be condemned: forgive, and ye shall be forgiven". My philosophy is not acceptance of a deviant lifestyle but a refusal to judge someone's behavior other than my own. Some people have difficulty understanding this.

It is becoming more and more apparent if you pay attention. Media includes television, movies, video games, newspapers and you even see these techniques in schools from kindergarten through college.

Young children deserve the opportunity to be children without this agenda being forced on them. Instead of concentrating on reading, writing and arithmetic emphasis is being placed on social studies. We can teach our children to be nice to others without bombarding them with sexuality, violence and dishonesty. While there are many excellent teachers, they are over shadowed by those pushing this agenda.

"Give me the child until the age of 12 and you can have him after that." As stated in American Education and

Indoctrination are Synonymous, by George Haddad*. He espouses many solid points showing how our children are being indoctrinated instead of educated. The National Education Association (NEA) has a stranglehold on our educational institutions. This organization controls teacher certification and has a great influence on curriculum. The NEA also exhibits great resistance to higher standards.

The NEA has led the charge in several western states attacking "home school" of students. The majority of those children who are home schooled appear to be more rounded in their education and have a greater grasp of reality. They are not subject to the polluted and distorted thinking and actions which are found in many public schools.

In many locations teachers are prevented from using red to correct student's papers. There are reports of students submitting mathematical answers which are wrong, i.e. 2+2=3 and not told they are wrong*. Malcolm X very accurately stated, "I'm sorry to say that the subject I most disliked was mathematics. I have thought about it. I think the reason was that mathematics leaves no room for argument. If you made a mistake that was all there was to it."

The elitists feel if red is used to correct wrong answers and a child is told their answer is wrong it may harm the self esteem of the child. It never hurt me, believe me, I saw a lot of red on my papers and the nuns who taught me were very quick to let me know when I had a wrong answer. No one is wrong or right all the time. I believe it is more of an injustice to not let someone know of their mistakes so they can have the opportunity to learn. Another quote these teachers should take note is from Samuel Smiles (1812-1904), "We learn wisdom from failure much more than from success. We often discover what will do by finding out what will not do; and probably he, who never made a mistake never made a discovery."

Florida legislatures recently took a bold step in passing education legislation with wording which states, American history* shall be "viewed as factual" not as "constructed." To a few social studies experts, the word "constructed" means interpretations (opinions) of history, and not being allowed to teach that would mean not being able to teach how ideas about historical events change over time. This is one of the main tools of the revisionists. These people fail to realize the facts of history do not change.

"History is not the facts but how those facts are interpreted," Theron Trimble, executive director of the

Florida Council for the Social Studies said, "Otherwise there would only be one history of the United States and no need for multiple textbooks or 25 books on the Civil War. History has to be revisited." In other words, history is the teacher's opinion of what history is despite the facts.

Here are a few examples of how the facts get in the way of history. Some Florida students believe Martin Luther King Jr. and Benjamin Franklin were presidents. Some believe the number of states count anywhere from 48 to 52. Many think the Declaration of Independence and Constitution is the same thing. I lived in Florida for awhile and saw a proposed textbook one of my children brought home. It actually had Christopher Columbus discovered America around 1500 A.D.! If this is what we get from the NEA our children are in more trouble than you can imagine. Take this flawed mentality and children who lack motivation and we have a recipe for disaster.

Many parents are to blame as well. You know the ones. Their child can do no wrong. This mentality exists in conservatives and liberals alike. The problem is it enables those with the agenda to weasel into legitimacy. I have first hand experience with this.

We have always been fair and honest with our children. When one of them had been accused of wrongdoing, I would investigate in order to validate. When I found my child to be in the wrong, they would be appropriately disciplined. While living in one particular neighborhood in Florida we were overwhelmed by all the other people's children who could do no wrong. We arrived home one day and as we rounded the turn we saw one of these little angels kicking over several of our yard ornaments. We pulled in the drive and he turned and looked at us and continued to kick over another one. When his mother was informed of this she stated, "Oh, no, my child couldn't do that". When she was informed we witnessed him first hand committing this act, she insisted we were mistaken. Needless to say this little angel was always in trouble in school as well.

Another good example of how the police may have gone a little too far and how a mother believes her child can do no wrong is the case in Florida. The video shows a little 5 year old exhibiting bad behavior*. Many elitists claim the little girl is hyperactive. The behavior I witnessed on the video is indicative of behavioral and lack of parental discipline not hyperactivity. After assaulting teachers and school administrators the police were called. When the police arrived the little girl was handcuffed and placed in the back of a patrol car. After awhile things settled down and everything returned to normal.

The mother's response was ""She's never going back to that school, they set my baby up." You may think this is the exception. I can assure you it is not.

Not all desensitizing is bad. After a cool reception of the movie "Look Who's Coming to Dinner" starring Sidney Poitier, Hollywood backed off for awhile. The sitcom "All in the Family" really helped change racial perspectives for the better. Unfortunately, much of the liberal media establishment use desensitization along with disinformation to further their agenda.

Look at other things that have been or are currently using desensitizing techniques. Remember the sitcom "Bewitched" starring Elizabeth Montgomery as a witch. It was a delightful comedy about a witch who was trying to live a normal life but inevitably ended up using "magic". It was very entertaining. An important note is you never saw a pentagram on this show. What do you think would have happened in the 1960s and 1970s if the show would have shown a pentagram? I believe it would not have gone over very well. Over the next couple of decades we were all exposed to small doses of witchcraft and Satanism.

This desensitization has culminated to what we have today. We have some entertaining television and movies from Hollywood that depicts evil as good.

41

These shows are fine for adults as we should know they should be accepted only as entertainment. Unfortunately, some adults don't and children are easily led. How in the world can someone believe there is evil fighting on the side of good? Let's start off with Buffy, the vampire slayer. Interesting, entertaining and unbelievably ridiculous! This show depicts the heroine fighting evil vampires and demons with the help of converted demons.

A spin-off of this show is another entertaining and ridiculous program called "Angel". This one has a vampire who has been cursed by a gypsy by having a soul. This soul comes with a conscience that forces Angel to know the difference between good and evil. Since he is different in this sense he hunts the evil vampires and demons to destroy them for good.

One of the more popular shows that seem to get a lot of attention, especially from young teenagers is "Charmed". As I stated earlier, these shows are fine for the attuned adult but not for the uniformed or young. This show is overflowing with witchcraft, demons and satanic rituals. The pentagram or other satanic symbol is displayed prominently throughout this show and the three "good" witches use it as a crutch to fight evil. Do you really think evil will fight evil? That's equivalent to believing Fidel Castro would have invaded Iraq to depose of Saddam Hussein to put a stop to the atrocities perpetrated against the Iraqi people.

If you know your children watch any of these shows, maybe you should sit down and watch these shows to see if you think its okay to expose them to this indoctrination. If you are true to your Christian, Judaism or Islam faith, it would be difficult to justify a young child watching programs such as these. Desensitizing a child to accept witchcraft and satanism lays the groundwork for indoctrination. Do you want your child falling into these beliefs? Did you know the U.S. Justice Department believes that satanism, Wicca and polytheism are religious beliefs?

The federal government argued in the Supreme Court* that states must enable prison inmates to practice and observe such "religious" beliefs — no matter how unconventional they may be. Desensitization has led to the mistaken belief these perversions are religious beliefs. I've not been able to find who made this quote but I believe it's very accurate for today. It goes something like this, "Satan's greatest accomplishment in the twentieth century is convincing people he did not exist". With the amount of movies, television shows and print media exhibiting witchcraft, satanic rituals and

43

pentagrams one would be hard pressed to deny this statement.

Desensitization has been very successful in the acceptance of gratuitous sex. Some people have become so distorted as to believe promiscuity is normal. Organizations such as Planned Parenthood appear to push a promiscuous lifestyle by promoting condom use and other contraception methods while either skipping or lightly addressing abstinence. The facts are teaching abstinence works. Abstinence was predominantly taught up until the 1970s. The rate of teenage pregnancy and out of wedlock pregnancy was significantly lower then than now*.

When was the last time you were able to watch a movie or television show without some kind of explicit sex scene? Even the modern cartoons exploit sex and other adult material children shouldn't be exposed to. Take the case of a father* who police arrested who refused to leave the Joseph Estabrook School after school officials rejected his demands that his 6-year-old son be shielded from any discussions about gay households. The 42 year old father, confronted officials after his son brought home "Who's in a Family", a storybook that includes characters who are gay parents. The man refused to leave a meeting after Lexington Superintendent rejected his demand that he be notified when his son is exposed to any discussion about same-sex households as part of classroom instruction. "Our parental requests for our own child were flat-out denied", Parker said in a statement.

Do you want the elitists deciding when and what your child will be exposed to? Are you willing to surrender your rights as a parent? The elitists have determined they know what's best for your child instead of you making the decision.

Another disturbing trend in desensitizing is pedophilia. We've all seen the recent cases especially in Florida. The only news network to bring these tragic events to the public eye seems to be Fox News Channel. The silence from the other news channels is deafening. Why are they not as interested in alerting the public about these ugly crimes? Could it be part of an uncoordinated desensitizing process by a lower power? You may ask, why anyone would want pedophilia to gain acceptance in America! Open your eyes and you may be amazed at what you've already began to tolerate and accept.

In 1994, the movie "The Professional" was released. The movie centered around Mathilda (played by Natalie Portman), a twelve-year old New York girl, living an undesirable life among her half-family. Her father stores drugs for a two-faced cop. Only her little brother keeps

Mathilda from breaking apart. One day, the cop and his team take cruel revenge on her father for stretching the drugs a little, thus killing the whole family. Only Mathilda, who was out shopping, survives by finding shelter in Léon's (Jean Reno) apartment in the moment of highest need. Soon, she finds out about the strange neighbor's unusual profession, killing, and desperately seeks his help in taking revenge for her little brother. Léon, who is completely inexperienced in fatherly tasks, and in friendships, does his best to keep Mathilda out of trouble, unsuccessfully. Now, the conflict between a killer, who slowly discovers his abilities to live, to feel, to love and a corrupt police officer, who does anything in his might to get rid of an eye witness, arises to immeasurable proportions, all for the sake of a little twelve-year old girl, who has nearly nothing to lose. Although there was no intimate contact the insinuation is similar to "The African Queen" with Humphrey Bogart and Katherine Hepburn. The "Professional" is a good movie but the underlying story of an illicit relationship is there.

Now, rocket forward about ten years. In 2004, the movie "Birth" starring Nicole Kidman as Anna a young widow who is finally getting on with her life after the death of her husband, Sean. Now engaged to be married, Anna meets a ten-year-old boy who tells her he is Sean reincarnated. Though his story is both unsettling and absurd, Anna can't get the boy out of her mind. And much to the concern of her fiancée, her increased contact with him leads her to question the choices she has made in her life. This doesn't sound so bad until you find out about a scene where they are together in a bathtub. Or the scene that's most disturbing is one which looks as if she is giving this ten year old a very passionate kiss. This is a kiss that an adult should never give a child.

Another item of interest is commercials. You may ask, "How in the world are commercials used to desensitize?" Think about it for a minute. Have you noticed the commercial for a male enhancement product to improve his sex life? When the commercials first started it would show the man making the phone call to order the product and then show the satisfied housewife after he began using the product. A series of commercials using this same couple appeared for awhile. Next it showed the couple with another couple and the other couple were not enjoying themselves until the first man gave his friend a tip to call for the male enhancement product. The commercial ended with both couples dancing around the living room. Sounds innocent enough but subconsciously the message could be targeted at "swinging". Now the commercials for this product show the man grilling food surrounded by his wife and several beautiful women while a group of other guys are shown painted up, drinking and hooting it up. For this one I asked my adult son what he took this to mean. He said it suggested this guy's wife was no longer enough for him and he "took care" of these other women indicating extramarital sex. Now we are seeing commercials for birth control and condoms presented in such a way as to promote promiscuity.

Do your own research about desensitization and open your eyes to what is going on around you. We all have become so accustomed to these distortions we are numb to the implications. Over the years Hollywood has bombarded us with perversions and distortions so much we are tolerating and accepting more and more. More and more you see women as the heroes and men the bad guys, crooks solving crimes to clear their names or their friends, bad guys working on the side of good by taking out corrupt cops. Take a good look at what Hollywood is producing. It used to be open season on white American males, now its open season on all American males and the traditional family.

"The trouble with fighting for human freedom is that one spends most of one's time defending scoundrels. For it is against scoundrels that oppressive laws are first aimed, and oppression must be stopped at the beginning if it is to be stopped at all." H. L. Mencken (1880 - 1956). Our government should not censure these so-called artistic endeavors but we as Christians, Jews, Islamist and other legitimate religions should send a message loud and clear and hit them in the pocketbook. We need to take a stand now before it's too late.

CHAPTER FOUR

The Great Deception

This is the most profound chapter concerning the acceptance of the subtle infringement on individual rights. While it is expected we trust our elected officials, the evidence dictates we should keep careful eye on their actions. These writings are meant to educate individuals as to the tricks many of these politicians as well as government bureaucrats are performing. As Thomas Jefferson states, "Enlighten the people, generally, and tyranny and oppressions of body and mind will vanish like spirits at the dawn of day." Each of us must take an active role to ensure excessive government is eliminated and officials work for our goals, not their own.

Everyone has heard "wolf in sheep's clothing" and "Trojan horse". Both phrases accurately describe many politicians today. Look and listen to these politicians during their campaign and their speeches after elected. Many tout moral values and traditional/conservative beliefs. Now take a look at their actual voting record and many times you will see a contradiction to what they have led you to believe where they stand. Both sides of the fence are guilty of this to a certain point.

Sometimes compromise is necessary in order to achieve some desired goals. These are not the ones I'm speaking about. You always know where the far right and far left stand. Then you have some who profess to be conservative or traditional in order to get elected. This happens to a great extent in the lower level of government such as county and municipal. Their deception causes more problems in our everyday lives as they operate under the radar of the national media and many exert considerable influence over the local media. Every once in a while the national media will pick up a story concerning these oppressive local governments.

Not all local media is prey to this political influence but many are. One small time news organization in the county where I live has yet to print any negative items concerning questionable actions of some of the commissioners. Many of the regulations infringing on individual rights, specifically private property, is ignored or sugar coated to lessen the negativity. Many of these small news outlets are used as tools to desensitize citizens to become more accepting of ridiculous zoning and so-called plans which restrict their rights. Local political propaganda abounds in some small town newspapers.

Imagine going to the voting booth and having only one choice on the ballot. This is reminiscing of the failed socialist society of the former Soviet Union. Here is a close rendition of what a ballot may have looked during the reign of communism there.

OFFICIAL BALLOT
STATE
RUSSIA, USSR

Shall the constitution, laws and the authority of the Politburo of U.S.S.R. be applicable to Russia in the U.S.S.R.?

YES (FOR CONSTITUTION AND LAW)

NO (AGAINST CONSTITUTION AND LAW)

Only those qualified electors residing outside municipal limits and in the country shall be permitted to vote or sign petition calling for the election in the state concerned.

END OF BALLOT

Take a close look at this ballot, beside where the yes and no is. Rather than read the whole ballot, human nature takes the easy way and reads only what is beside the yes and no. Most sane people would vote yes, After all, who wouldn't vote favorably for a constitution extolling freedoms and laws that protect the citizens from excessive government?

Now compare this ballot, which, is exactly the same wording used in an Alabama County in January 2005.

OFFICIAL BALLOT

CHELSEA NORTH–
DUNNAVANT VALLEY SOUTH–
WESTOVER NORTH
ZONING BEAT ELECTION
JANUARY 18, 2005

Shall the zoning regulations, the master plan and the authority of the Planning Commission of Shelby County, Alabama be applicable to the Chelsea North — Dunnavant Valley South — Westover North Zoning Beat of Shelby County, Alabama?

YES(FOR ZONING REGULATIONS)

NO(AGAINST ZONING REGULATIONS)

Only those qualified electors residing outside municipal limits and in the unzoned portion of the beat shall be permitted to vote or sign petition calling for the election in the beat concerned.

END OF BALLOT

On the surface, this ballot doesn't appear unreasonable. What if you want zoning, but not the authority of the planning commission? You may ask, why not? You need a little history in order to understand the significance of this which we will delve into later in the paragraphs ahead. The planning commission members are not elected by the electorate. This misleads people into thinking they are voting to give authority to the elected county commissioners. The major problem with voting to give authority to the "planners" is they are not held accountable to anyone. Once the electorate gives them the authority they can then change zoning regulations to whatever they feel and the electorate has no recourse. Essentially, in a case such as this, the electorate has forever given away any control they could have over zoning of their community to a group that doesn't have to answer for anything they may decide which may adversely affect the citizens in this area.

Remember, although this is focusing on a specific county in a specific state, similar situations are occurring throughout the United States.

In Colorado, after passage of Sustainable Comprehensive Zoning Plan, local governments condemned property owners "current use" (those who were grandfathered in at time of zoning) and after an amortization period the government declared ownership! The State Legislature's effort to alleviate the undesired effects of property condemnation resulted in the enactment of "Concerning a prohibition on the use by local governments of amortization to eliminate nonconforming uses of property". This legislation can be viewed at the State's web site www.state.co.us!

In Oregon a Sustainable Comprehensive Zoning Plan was passed. As a direct result of the restrictive sustainable zoning regulations, angry citizens voted on an amendment (Measure 7) in 2000 to override the Sustainable Comprehensive Zoning Plan. Due to a technicality, a State Judge overturned it. A second attempt to override the Sustainable Comprehensive Zoning, called Measure 37*, was again voted on and passed in 2004 by the citizens who angry at being deceived in the original Sustainable Comprehensive Zoning. This time the voice of the citizens cannot be overturned by a judge who attempts to legislate from the bench. This legislation can be viewed at the State's web site www.state.or.us!

The local politicians and the American Planning Association are in a tizzy over this. I believe this was posted but has since been removed from their website. "The Real Story Behind Measure 37*. Last November, Oregon voters approved Measure 37 through an initiative based more on public relations than public information. Now residents are beginning to discern the true costs of this unfair manifestation of the so-called "property rights" movement".

These organizations perceive anything pertaining to individual rights (notice "so-called 'property rights' movement" with a negative slant above) as an obstacle to their agenda, henceforth, the attacks. Notice the residents rose to the occasion and decided to take the matter in their own hands instead of letting these socialists take away their rights. Citizen activism, such as this, is a major setback for these "planners". Residents are the ones informed and the public relations disinformation scam is usually performed by the "planners". When citizens are armed with the truth they can count on always being attacked and their view distorted from the ones pushing this socialistic agenda. These "planners" are often aided by the liberal media.

Let's get back to the County in Alabama. The State Legislature originally passed legislation in 1982 to establish a "Shelby County Planning Commission" to afford the county limited structure to govern the county in relation to zoning and development. Over the past couple of years members of the Commission have persuaded the State Legislature to pass an Amendment to the State's Constitution granting the Commission widespread power far exceeding what is healthy for the citizens of this county. The citizens of the county did not lobby for this and were misinformed about the intent of the Amendment when the vote took place.

The original intent of forming this Planning Commission was to develop reasonable zoning for the booming housing development taking place and planning economic development within the county. The Commission has managed to far exceed this intent. Ronald Reagan said it best, "Man is not free unless government is limited… As government expands liberty contracts."

The Commission now has total control over all county government as well as developing zoning plans and control of commerce. They manipulated the State Legislature to modify Alabama Act 82-693 Section 8. 6th sentence to read, "The ballot shall be so worded as to give the voter the opportunity to vote either 'Yes' or 'No' as to whether the voter wishes the authority of the Commission, its master plan, and the zoning regulations to apply to the beat".

Zoning isn't so bad, but the master plan violates the United State's Constitution and the Constitution of Alabama and the authority of the Commission exceeds the needs of the county. The Shelby County Sustainable

Comprehensive Zoning Plan can best be viewed at www.shelbycitizen.org! This site gives you insight into the intent of this plan and provides a glossary so you can check the meaning of words and phrases. This is something the Shelby County website did not do until after the vote.

The collective framework of this plan smacks any freedom loving person in the face. A good example of this can be found in Section II page 3 of the plan. It states, "Recognize the private property rights of the individual within a balanced framework that considers the public interest and **SHARED** values of the **COMMUNITY**". While this sounds good and is supported by touting traditional neighborhoods with walkable communities it abounds with socialism and collectivism. In simple language, the use of your property is whatever the County Commissioners determine your property would be best suited for.

Shelby County's Sustainable Comprehensive Zoning Plan* contains, most probably the most ridiculous infringement on page II-6:"Well head protection" which means any water you remove from a creek, private well, or even rain water, which creates surface water on your property, that, when diverted or collected must be measured (lakes, irrigation ponds, etc…) with the possibility of you paying for it! Sounds absurd? Look at what happened in the state of Washington.

Washington State passed "Well head protection" in 1993 called "Water Measuring Devices, Metering of Diversions Law." You can read about this at www.ecy.wa.gov/programs/wr/measuring/meas uringhome.html! Initially this law was not enforced because of how ridiculous it is as Washington is almost equivalent to the Biblical Noah's Ark environment. Seven years later, March 2000, a suit was filed against Washington's Department of Enforcement to force it to comply with the law passed in 1993. The state had to comply because it was the law. This lawsuit and ruling reflects a "predetermined outcome". The politicians passed this law knowing it wouldn't be popular and a few years down the road this would happen to force implementation. They could have fixed this before this lawsuit but the politicians wanted this to happen, thus, predetermined outcome.

Another item of concern should raise red flags in the Shelby County Plan. Section Three page 13 of the plan states, "Develop and implement a separate Land Disturbance Ordinance, applicable to all unincorporated land in Shelby County with appropriate penalties, and consistent with the goals, objectives and policies of this comprehensive plan." Companies which are behind these plans, write something like this so as not bring attention to what they actually mean.

Once developed and implemented the statement's intent is, if you own land in the unincorporated area of the County you won't be able to trim your shrubs, clear some underbrush, trim or prune a tree or even cut one down, excavate or grade your property without getting permission from the planning commission. The plan also states approval will be "costly (markedly higher fees) and lengthy" so as to regulate and frustrate to cause you to stop or conform your plans. If you live in a "special district" this will have little impact on residential neighborhoods unless, of course, you have a few acres, typically an estate, farm or ranch.

Can you imagine, here in America, the local government has to grant you permission to remove that big 100 year old oak tree which was blown down in the last storm and then making you pay for a permit once permission is granted? Basically, you are stripped of your personal property rights. The Bible states in Genesis 1:26 — "And God said, Let us make man in our image, after our likeness: and let them have dominion over the fish of the sea, and over the fowl of the air, and over the cattle, and over **all the earth**, and over every creeping thing that creepeth upon the earth". The Koran and Book of Bereishith in the Torah reflect similar statements. God gave us, the individual, stewardship over the land. I don't see commissioner, representative, judge, mayor, governor or government anywhere in the scriptures where God grants us dominion (rights).

Another thing you should know about this vote. Several housing developments are located in the beat where this vote took place. These areas have been designated "special districts" by the County Commissioners and have their own zoning rules. Many of these residents were told the zoning within the beat they were located would not affect them only the unincorporated areas outside these "special districts". They were given assurances this zoning would protect their property value and control the other properties so no one could "build a hog farm next door to them.

This MO is used to deceive people into supporting a flawed plan. First, these areas already have zoning that prevents someone from building a hog farm in their subdivision. Second, the commission already has the jurisdiction to prevent a hog farm from being placed close to a subdivision. The most disturbing item concerning this vote is people who are supposedly not affected by this zoning were allowed to vote on measures that affect others and not themselves. All the people residing in the unincorporated areas and outside these "special districts" must now abide by zoning voted in by these affluent areas while they, the affluent, are not affected.

In 1215 AD, King John implemented the Magna Carta that ended the Feudal System where the haves dictated to the have-nots how they were to use their land. In the late 17th century the colonies in North America adopted these laws and the U.S. Constitution is based on this. After almost eight hundred years of the Magna Carta's implementation and almost two hundred thirty years of the U.S. Constitution existence, we are seeing the return of the Feudal System of government. Instead of lords they are now called elitists. Some may even call the local elitist leader commissioner.

The preceding are just a very few of the numerous infringements in this one Sustainable Comprehensive Zoning Plan. If you live in an area, county or parish and attempts are made to implement a plan such as this, read it before you vote on it. If you love freedom and individual rights you'll make the right decision. As for your commissioners, if they support any plan which infringes on your rights, vote them out of office. Remember, there is a reason they are called commissioner and not representative. They do not represent you, they are to carry out your will and abide by the Constitution and laws of the State. They are **not** there to represent you to your State Legislature!

It will only be a matter of time before these commissioners lobby the State Legislature for powers reserved for representatives.

You may be asking who could possibly be behind this type of plan? There are many organizations who promote these plans. One company, KPS Group*, is proud of pushing the Sustainable Comprehensive Zoning Plan in Shelby County since they were instrumental in its development. It's sugarcoated in such a way many readers misunderstand much of the restrictive language. This Group even nominated this specific plan for a top award by the Alabama Chapter of the American Planning Association. Although this association has been around for about ninety years it began to slide toward promoting the stripping away of individual property ownership rights only a few years ago.

The Plan claims to have been in the works for over a year. KPS Group held at least two workshops to "educate" citizens who were involved in the development of these plans. These citizens thought they had constructive input but it appears they were manipulated and steered toward a predetermined outcome. After studying and listening to how this so-called citizen involvement occurred I believe the planners may have used a technique called the "Delphi Process" a RAND Corp. development. It's a technique used to falsely reach a "consensus" within a group when a person manipulates the group. This technique, when used effectively, will guarantee a predetermined outcome.

You don't have to look far to see where these companies are taking their cue. Take for example a statement in the preamble of a Document on the Conference of Human Settlement Recommendation D.5 (C)(V). "Land…cannot be treated as an ordinary asset, controlled by individuals and subject to the pressures and inefficiencies of the market…Private land ownership is also a principal instrument of accumulation and concentration of wealth, and, therefore, contributes to social injustice; if left unchecked, it may become a major obstacle in the planning and implementation of development schemes (The meaning of schemes is a crafty or secret plan or program of action; plot; intrigue). The provision of decent dwelling and healthy conditions for the people can only be achieved if land is used in society as a whole. Public Control of land use is therefore indispensable…" Further information can be found on the website: http://sovereignty.freedom.org/p/land/unp roprts.htm! This reeks of socialism. All freedom loving Americans should take note of how your elected officials are supporting or not supporting individual rights issues. You must be careful in how you present your argument. In my experience I've noticed when a liberal (individual or organization, i.e. ACLU) talks about individual rights, it is perceived as looking out for the people. When a conservative (individual or group) talks about individual rights they are immediately classified as part of a militia or subversive.

Unfortunately, many of the local politicians, of both major parties, claim to be conservative but their actions denote socialism as evidenced by many of these Sustainable Comprehensive Zoning Plans. This great deception is leading this nation down the path of ruin which is reflected not only in this matter but moral issues as well.

Many private organizations contribute to this deception. Some are essentially fronts for wealthy socialists. Take moveon.org* for example! This website has received millions of dollars from George Soros. Soros has made billions of dollars trading currency. It is reported he has given billions of dollars over the years to promote democracy around the world. According to news reports he is a self avowed liberal who has his own vision for America and the world. He promotes what is known as the Open Society*. He is pushing the socialist agenda throughout the world and claiming to spread democracy. He funded anti-conservative activities through many 527s (an organization that is created to receive and disburse funds to influence or attempt to influence the nomination, election, appointment or defeat of candidates for public office). Moveon.org is one of these organizations.

The deception listed by this organization is unbelievable to say the least. From distorting the facts about social security to false information concerning the Iraq war. Claims of infringements on Americans liberties from the Patriot Act have proven to be unfounded but that doesn't stop the propaganda. While I strongly believe it is our duty to hold our elected officials accountable I also believe there is a line we cannot step over before it is considered treasonous. Although these 527s actions are questionable and may not have stepped over the line George Soros may have. As stated in the United States Constitution "Article III. Section 3. Treason against the United States, shall consist only in levying War against them, or in adhering to their Enemies, giving them Aid and Comfort". Dissent against the war is one thing. Attacking the President and the United States Military in a way to provide propaganda for the enemy is quiet another. Endangering the lives of our troops and other Americans is treason!

Apparently one of the most favored organizations the elitists like to push is the American Association of Retired

People (AARP). Take a look at these facts:

Fact #1: In 1994 AARP was forced in a settlement with the U.S. Internal Revenue Service to pay $135 million dollars.

Fact #2: The AARP made it possible for Social Security benefits to be taxed — first in 1984 then again in 1993 by refusing to work to eliminate this tax.

Fact #3: The AARP allowed for Social Security payroll tax increases on hardworking Americans (more than 18 over the last four decades)

Fact #4: The AARP was taking millions in taxpayer dollars to help fund their operations (more than $1 BILLION dollars in taxpayer money in just the last 14 years!)

It's hard to imagine how any person or organization would even think they could get away without paying their fair share of taxes while sitting idle when everyone else's taxes were being raised and while actually taking money paid by hardworking and law abiding taxpayers.

It doesn't stop there for the AARP. Their commercials distort the Presidents plan for Social Security. This organization is artistically using scare tactics on the elderly. According to them the President's plan calls for cutting their benefits. The facts are if you are over 55 years old your benefits will not be affected. According to Thomas R. Saving, in a *Statement before the Senate Special Committee on Aging*, July 29,

2003, "If nothing is done to Social Security today it will beginning in 2008 and in all subsequent years, become a drag on the federal budget… Today, Social Security and Medicare account for only 35 percent of federal expenditures. By 2060, the two programs will require more than 71 percent of the federal budget". This directly contradicts the stand taken by the AARP.

The elitists and many Democrats claim there is no Social Security crisis. This was not their belief when these remarks were made by President Bill Clinton, At Georgetown University On Social Security, Washington, DC, 2/9/98, on: "If you don't do anything, one of two things will happen, either it will go broke and you won't ever get it, or if we wait too long to fix it, the burden on society … of taking care of our generation's social security obligations will lower your income and lower your ability to take care of your children to a degree that most of us who are parents think would be horribly wrong and unfair to you and unfair to the future prospects of the United States." This is not the only time President Clinton addressed the crisis for Social Security. In his State Of The Union, January 19, 1999 he said, "First, and above all, we must save Social Security for the 21st Century."

This isn't an issue on Social Security but on how the elitists think and act.

This is meant to demonstrate the deceptive techniques and the measures of which the people will go to push their agenda. When their man (President Clinton) said there was a crisis with Social Security it had to be true but when the other side mentions it, a different story emerges. When the mention of personal accounts was brought up the elitists went crazy. The elitist crowd said Social Security is supposed to provide enough income for one to live on. Imagine what the outrage they felt when they heard this statement, "It is proposed that the Federal Government assume one-half of the cost of the old-age pension plan, which ought **ultimately to be supplanted by self-supporting annuity plans**". Can't you just hear President George Bush say these words? Well, President Franklin Roosevelt spoke these words in his message to Congress on Social Security. January 17,1935.

One can clearly see the distortions of the facts by these elitists. Granted, both sides try to slant the argument in their favor, but the far left doesn't let facts get in their way as evidenced by the above. The AARP is so adept at this I believe they should change their moniker in a way to keep their acronym to reveal what they do best. This organization would best be described as **A**merican **A**ssociation of **R**idiculous **P**ropaganda. I believe this would be more fitting for this organization.

CHAPTER FIVE

We The People,
They The Government?

Once upon a time, about forty years ago, a Democrat by the name of Lyndon Johnson was president of the United States. He had this grand idea of a Great Society where the less fortunate, undereducated and impoverished needed a hand-up. At this time the Democrat party was the party of the people. Then along came the bad little socialist. They saw an opportunity to create a voter base by embellishing the programs meant to give a hand-up into programs giving a handout. They could, in turn, use this entitlement mentality to further their agenda. Slowly, infiltration began throughout all levels of the government and all avenues of the media.

Suddenly, there was a technology explosion which helped to educate the citizens. The people slowly began to realize what they thought was the party of the people was no longer true. The Republicans more accurately reflect the average American. The masses demanded welfare reform during the nineties and congress and the president reluctantly complied. The extremists are still trying hard but are now using other methods to further their agenda.

The beginning of the United States Constitution reads, "We the People". Over the past fifty years, or thereabouts, the socialists have managed to turn this into "We the Government". To give you an understanding of how severe this has become, look at the amount of laws that have been passed since 1960. About 4 times more federal laws have been passed in this time than the preceding 175 years of this Country's existence. This doesn't take into account the state and local laws. Granted, some of these laws are needed but most are not.

The Great Society envisioned by President Lyndon Johnson had many good ideals which made it appealing to the majority of Americans. No American wanted to see any of their countrymen in poverty. I grew up in the fifties and sixties in a low income area. I witnessed my parents giving to others when they didn't have enough for us. A helping hand was always there for all Americans. My dad helped as many minorities as any other group of people. He was the first generation in America as his parents migrated to find a better life as most immigrants do.

We lived in a very diverse area of town which may surprise many people as we lived in the Heart of Dixie. I guess to the wealthy and self righteous, we lived on the "other side of the tracks". In 1965, the Great Society came to be. Kids, who were my friends, were no longer. We were considered white and many of them were of a different race. Although we experienced some divisions before then, we usually came around and continued this friendship. But then, it happened!

Most of the hard working older men continued to work hard to provide for their families. Many programs were implemented to help these families exit poverty, which was good. We didn't receive any of this help but many of my friends families did. It didn't change their parents but it did change them. Suddenly, they expected to receive money from the government. I remember hearing a Democrat politician state in a speech, "Look at what I've given to you". I remember other politicians reflect similar statements such as, "Look at what I've done for you". What started as a noble venture turned into the establishment of a voter base many of who expected a handout.

Those who were impoverished, undereducated and hard working at first, saw hope. These parents witnessed many of their children believing they no longer had to work hard as their parents as they would be taken care of by the government. This seemed to solidify a hard core voter base which primarily consisted of minority Democrats.

The elite media did their part in bias reporting of stories. I remember witnessing events only to see the media distort the facts which misled the viewers. By the end of the sixties, there were only three major networks and all three began their slant to the left.

I've talked with many people about their political leanings and after checking occupational statistics came to a startling conclusion. Many middle age and older people registered as Democrat continue to vote straight Democrat regardless of who is running. You do not see as much of this with registered Republicans. Most of these registered Democrats were members of labor unions and some were minorities and many others were undereducated. These people were easily manipulated and even today many feel they are pressured or manipulated to vote the Democratic ticket.

About fifteen years ago I was discussing an upcoming election with an uncle of mine. He worked the steel mills all his life and was hardcore union member. He was a lifelong Democrat as well as NRA member. I asked him what his views were on taxes, government programs, abortion and gun control. His response reflected those of the Republicans. When I told him this, he refused to accept it. I told him the measures many elected Democrats were taking to restrict guns with the intention of banning them in the end. He accused me of not being truthful. He stated he always voted straight Democrat and wouldn't change now. He thought the Party still reflected the philosophy of Hubert Humphrey.

In the following years came the advent of cable news, conservative talk radio and various other media outlets that provided equal time for the conservative word to get out. Shortly before the 2000 presidential elections I was fortunate enough to have a similar discussion with this uncle concerning the same topics from about ten years earlier. When I asked him if he was voting for Al Gore, he replied, "I wouldn't vote for that jerk if my life depended on it". When I asked why he wasn't voting the Democrat ticket like he always did, he said that since he retired he had managed to keep abreast of events and where these politicians stand. He was not happy with the direction the Democrat Party is heading.

As recent as last year (2004) I talked with several members of a labor union. These guys said their shop steward repeatedly told them they had better vote for John Kerry because if Bush got reelected they most probably would get laid off. They said other higher ups in the union even mentioned things like this in meetings with other members. The threats and intimidation by some unions appear to be criminal.

The average IQs* of registered members of political parties is surprising to say the least. Many undereducated still remain susceptible to influence and intimidation. Democrats average IQ fall into the range of 110, Republicans average IQ is around 120, while Independents is above 130. What does this mean? Easy, the more educated you become the more you can think for yourself and have a greater tendency to resist undue influence. Unfortunately, many of the institutions of higher learning are indoctrinating students into the elitist mentality. While many of the Democrat elitists exhibit a higher IQ the bulk of their followers do not.

Thanks to the explosion in cable news and internet outlets people are being exposed to more information. This enables many of these people to make more informed decisions. Because of this availability of information the socialists are getting desperate. You are now seeing more deceptive techniques used as in so-called public safety issues, indoctrination in our schools and restrictive regulations.

The appearance of one of the more atrocious abuses of a voter base by the Democrats used in recent years is the Black population. I've had political discussions with numerous minorities over the past few years. I don't know what the problem is, but, after lengthy discussions, I've found many people of the black population still exhibit the Great Society mentality. This mentality seems to be fostered by some of the old school civil rights leaders. They seem to be taking advantage of the poor while they enrich themselves.

Almost all the Republicans who are black I've talked with appear to be well informed and discern information and make their own decisions concerning politics. After talking with a large number of black people who profess to be Democrat, I can safely say about ten percent are well informed and make sound political decisions based on solid information. To put the impact of this in perspective about ten percent of the black population voted Republican and another ten percent voted Democrat based on educated decisions and who would best represent their views. This leaves approximately eighty percent who do not base their vote on solid information but emotion.

The elitists love this because most of their arguments concerning most important topics are emotional. So you can now see the manipulation of this group of people. If you are one who doesn't believe this to be true here is a prediction for you. If Condoleezza Rice, J.C. Watts or Colin Powell is on the Republican ticket in 2008 or 2012 watch the percentage of black voters rise for the Republicans. I may be wrong about this. I believe the elitist's manipulation of emotion in this segment of population will backfire. Let's wait and see!

To see further manipulation of the political process look at the recent elections. In the 2000 presidential election the liberals were the group who took the matter to the courts. Instead of waiting for the voter's final decision they wanted the activist courts to decide the election. When the Bush team decided enough was enough, they took it to the Supreme Court which upheld the rule of law. That was a thorn in the socialists' side. Independent news agencies flooded the counties in Florida and over the following months managed to perform independent recounts of their own. Even though most news organizations exhibited a liberal slant, they performed their recount fairly and all recounts still showed President Bush the winner.

Now, let's take a look at the November 2004 Presidential Election. Accusations from the left concerning voter irregularities in Ohio* were investigated and the final count adjusted to reflect an accurate count showing the President still winning by 119,000 votes. Accusations still persisted and several investigations were conducted and most questions were answered and/or clarified for the most part. While questions of some voter irregularities remain there are not near enough to change the course of the election. That didn't stop the hard core elitists from attempting to delay the validation of the vote in congress.

Let's jump to Washington State Gubernatorial election. The Republican candidate won by a slim margin. Two recounts ordered show he still won. The Democrat candidate demanded another recount which reflected her as the winner. Margin of victory was about 129. Several investigations, some of which were independent, confirmed significant irregularities and voter fraud.

Here's the deal. In Ohio, out of approximately 7.5 million votes, Bush won by 119,000 for a margin of 1.5 percent. The hardcore dems want a recount and investigations. In the State of Washington with approximately 3 million votes, the Democrat Governor won by 129 votes for a margin of .00043 percent. The hardcore dems say that's final. I've seen some of the evidence in Washington and not surprised by the activist judges sitting on their hands on this one.

Many of the elitists in and out of the government are guilty of "group think". This is when everyone they associate with, thinks the same way they do. Being surrounded by those who think, act and live as you do places one in a very narrow focus and leads to the false assumption the majority of the population thinks the same way. How many times have you heard "flyover country"? This term was coined by the elitists to describe the majority of the land mass in the United States between the east and west coast. As far as they think only people living in New England, Atlanta, Miami, San Francisco, Los Angeles and a few other major cities are educated and informed enough to understand what the country's needs are.

I've heard many elitists use this phrase especially during the 2004 elections. They seemed to be astounded when the "flyover country hicks" defeated them with a resounding voice. You see, these elitists failed to realize that almost 200 million people live in flyover country. These elitists live in these densely populated areas with millions of people and erroneously think they make up the majority of the country. Some of those with the elitist mentality have migrated to "flyover" areas of the country. This infiltration is detrimental to our society as it appears to contradict the basic fabric that has made America great.

This country is founded on rural living and is one of the most mentally and physically healthy environments for a child to be raised in. Take this example of how the elitist mentality in bureaucratic agencies affects our society and views rural living with disdain. A couple in Juntura, Oregon with a population of about 50, had been childless for 15 years. After repeatedly being turned down by adoption agencies, this couple had resigned themselves to remaining childless*. The reason given by a caseworker, "the lack of cultural opportunities on a ranch"! A family friend told them to contact a lawyer in Boise, Idaho who was a parent to an adopted Haitian child. In 1994 after a short time they adopted three Haitian children from 7 months to 2 ½ years old. In 1996 the couple adopted 3 more Haitian children. Although one of the children was high strung and exhibited disruptive behavior the couple refused to put him on Ritalin as most school systems would do. Instead they put him on a horse. The children are schooled at home and according to the adopted mother, "realizes the value of the ranch as a rich educational source." These children are excelling in their lives as well as education. Although the community and the parents are white, the children are viewed no differently than other children and are admired as polite, smart, honest and good ranch hands.

Thanks to the couples friend advising them to work around the "group think" system they are now happy and have heirs to a ranch they have put their blood and sweat into. Think for a minute though. If these children were left to their fate in a Haitian orphanage how they would survive and how they would turn out. No thanks to the elitists in the system, these children were most likely rescued from a life of misery. The parents now have an opportunity to leave a lasting legacy.

These elitists "feel" rather than think. This leads to abuses of power as well as destruction of our republican form of government.

Remember during the 2000 presidential elections when Al Gore and Lynn Chaney were on Fox News? I believe this was before Al Gore received the Democratic nomination. Although not an official debate the differences were crystal clear. When the question of violence in the media, i.e. Hollywood and music, Al Gore said he believed the government should place controls over what Hollywood and music producers could produce in order to protect the children from the violent influence. Lynn Chaney's response was "If you don't like it, change the channel"! This is a good indicator of who wants to infringe on your freedoms. The elitists think they know what is best for you. Just think, many of these people are in government and/or positions of influence. If a moderate or conservative made a statement similar to Mr. Gore's, what do you think the repercussions would be? We'd here about it in the news for weeks of how the conservative politicians want to take your freedoms.

Over the years the government has been unduly influenced by special interest groups rather than the average citizens. The elitist would agree with this statement but they would be thinking about the National Rifle Association or some of the pro-life organizations. They wouldn't consider Moveon.org (sponsored by billionaires), Planned Parenthood (sponsored by many "pro-choice" organizations) and the many more organizations comprised of wealthy and/or businesses. These elitists don't understand the NRA and pro-life groups are comprised of normal everyday citizens not big business or the filthy rich with an agenda to control the direction of this country you see with groups like Moveon.org and Planned Parenthood.

Elitists feel the government should dictate as well as control our lives. For example take eminent domain. Originally, eminent domain was adopted by our government to provide for responsible development of roadways and bridges. This is taken from Wikipedia, the free encyclopedia. "In law, eminent domain is the power of the state to appropriate private property for its own use without the owner's consent. Governments most commonly use the power of eminent domain when the acquisition of real property is necessary for the completion of a public project such as a road, and the owner of the required property is unwilling to negotiate a price for its sale."

In the United States, the Fifth Amendment to the Constitution requires that just compensation be paid when the power of eminent domain is used, and requires that "public purpose" of the property be demonstrated. Over the course of the last century and especially the last 40 years eminent domain has been perverted to include in the definition of "public purpose" as economic development schemes which use eminent domain to displace private homes and businesses in order to transfer it to private developments that are more profitable. These local governments also are failing to pay just compensation. Instead of "fair market value" or "just value" these officials, with complicity of lower courts, are managing to pay many property owners the assessed value of their property. For a better understanding or how this is swindling property owners take a look at your property tax notice and look at the "assessed value" used to assess your property taxes. Now take a look at the fair market value of your property. You will see the fair market value as anywhere from 5 to 10 times more than the assessed value. These officials are getting away with this because most of the property owners are not wealthy people and cannot afford to fight this.

Take the case as reported on FNC February 22, 2005*. The town of New London, Connecticut attempted to misuse eminent domain to acquire several homes for a river walk, townhouses and a hotel. By taking these peoples homes they could greatly increase their tax revenue. They had little regard for the citizens who lived in these homes. The officials had dollar signs in their eyes. The thing that made this worse was one of the families were forced out of their home by the local government about 30 years before under the guise of building a seawall. Its been 30 years and the seawall has not yet materialized.

Take another example about a weeklong eminent domain trial in Cincinnati, Ohio, that took place in April*. Scott Bullock, Attorney for The Institute for Justice, wrote, "This case concerns a challenge to another bogus "blight" designation of a perfectly fine middle-class neighborhood of homes and small, locally owned businesses. In this case, a developer, who has $500,000,000 in assets, wishes to expand two shopping plazas that he already owns by building "Rookwood Exchange," a complex of private office buildings, high-end apartments and chain stores in Norwood (a suburb of Cincinnati). A group of home and business owners refused to sign contracts with Anderson; they instead simply wanted to keep what was rightfully theirs".

He continued on, "When the developer was unable to obtain the properties voluntarily, he asked Norwood's City Council to pursue an urban renewal study of the area to see if the neighborhood was "blighted." This developer demanded and paid for the study and, on the basis of this work, the City absurdly declared that the neighborhood was "blighted/deteriorated" and "deteriorating."

Mr. Bullock continues, "Of course, the blight designation was a fraud. The study admitted none of the homes was dilapidated or delinquent on taxes. And the supposed problems with the neighborhood, such as the design of the streets and the increased traffic from the near-by developments, were created either by the City or the developer's other projects."

"Everyone knows why the study was done: in Ohio, you need an urban renewal plan in order to condemn property for redevelopment. Adding to the charade, the developer agreed to reimburse the City for the costs of acquiring the property and agreed to pay the City's legal fees if the eminent domain case went to trial. Thus, the City rented out its eminent domain authority—one of the most awesome powers government has at its disposal—to a private party. Call it government by the highest bidder…!"

The Institute for Justice continues the fight for citizens and businesspeople willing to stand up and fight for their rights so the scourge of eminent domain abuse will be eliminated.

For a better look at the special interests which most influence our political process, you can look at hierarchy of the American Bar Association* (founded on August 21,1878, in Saratoga Springs, New York, by 100 lawyers from 21 states) and the American Medical Association* (Nathan S. Davis MD Founded AMA at Academy of Natural Sciences in Philadelphia in 1847). Both of which are laden with elitists. The leadership of these two organizations is at many times at odds with their general membership.

While there are many good lawyers there are those who wish to influence the direction of this country. The ABA is responsible for establishing many of the requirements for one to practice law in this country. There are many people who are intelligent and self taught who are capable of passing their state bar exam but aren't allowed because they never attended or completed an accredited law school. If one is capable of passing the bar why, then, are they not allowed to practice law? One answer is the individual will be well versed in constitutional law and not indoctrinated into the far left views of law.

A good example of this indoctrination can be seen in the lawyers who represent the American Civil Liberties Union (ACLU). This organization no longer is looking after the rights of the individual but appears to embrace many of the socialistic philosophies inherent of the elitists. This is straight from the ACLU's website:

"The mission of the ACLU is to preserve all of these protections and guarantees:

• Your First Amendment rights-freedom of speech, association and assembly. Freedom of the press, and freedom of religion supported by the strict separation of church and state."

This appears to be well and good but, in fact is very misleading. The exact wording of the First Amendment to the U.S. Constitution is as follows:

"Congress shall make no law respecting an establishment of religion, or prohibiting the free exercise thereof; or abridging the freedom of speech, or of the press, or the right of the people peaceably to assemble, and to petition the Government for redress of grievances."

No where does it say in the United States Constitution "separation of church and state". It does state as above, the government will not establish a specific religion. If you read the Federalists Papers, you will see the founding fathers did not want our government to mimic Great Britain as they established the Church of England (Anglican). If you really want to take a good look at where the ACLU developed their idea about separation of church and state you'll find it in the former Soviet Union's Constitution, originally adopted in 1917 and reaffirmed in 1925 and finally October 7, 1977*.

"Article 52 [Religion]

(1) Citizens of the USSR are guaranteed freedom of conscience, that is, the right to profess or not to profess any religion, and to conduct religious worship or atheistic propaganda. Incitement of hostility or hatred on religious grounds is prohibited. (2) **In the USSR, the church is separated from the state, and the school from the church.**" (Emphasis mine)

By applying the above a clear line is drawn by the constant attacks by the ACLU on religion, religion in schools and organizations promoting religious faith such as the Boy Scouts. I believe the acronym ACLU should change its moniker to more accurately reflect what this organization actually promotes. **A**mericans **C**an't **L**ive **U**nimpeded!

The AMA is not much better. My specialty in the military consisted of extensive training in medicine. While there were many medics, nurses and doctors, there were only a few in my field of expertise. We were trained as independent duty medical personnel. The training was much more extensive than a paramedic. Essentially we were trained to be a hospital rolled into one person because we operated in the field with no other medical personnel. Many of us in this field continued our education in order to provide better care for the troops we deployed with. Unfortunately, some did not expand this training. Anyway, I know of a few of these people who became certified in every medical procedure available to them as well as attending numerous physician in-service training. Several of these guys became Advanced Cardiac Life Support instructors who taught physicians and nurses on advanced life support techniques and procedures. Some of them were more knowledgeable and proficient than some general practice physicians.

One, in particular, was on par with many physicians. He deployed on an extended remote tour in a third world country of which one of his primary jobs was to perform civic action in the form of medical care to the local population. He had to be "certified" by the local government's Director of Public Health. The Director's initial review of his record impressed him and he offered the medic the opportunity to take his country's medical boards for family practice. He jumped on this opportunity and had several weeks to prepare. This country was a territory of the United States and the boards were administered by American Physicians and were of the same standard held by many of the states in the U.S.! He performed as well or better than the local medical school graduates and became board certified in that country. Upon return from this assignment he kept current on all his training and took advantage of every opportunity to gain more experience. Several of the people who took the boards the same time he did traveled to the United States and were allowed to take the medical boards in the state they traveled to. This was promising since he was board certified in their country as they were. After a few years he left the military and was interested in challenging the boards in his state. Unfortunately, he did not meet the states criteria thanks to the requirement of graduating from an accredited medical school. This is thanks to the AMA. This man even called the local medical school and asked if he could challenge their curriculum tests to prove he was capable. The dean's office stated he could if he paid the full 4 year tuition. He could not come up with well over a hundred thousand dollars.

While I don't advocate just anybody walking in off the street to challenge the state bar or medical boards there should be exceptions. Thanks to the elitists in the ABA and AMA influencing government agencies exceptions will never occur. When this man stated, if he could afford it, if he had to pay full tuition he may as well attend the school. The assistant's reply summed it all up, "That's what we prefer so we can teach you our philosophy". This man knew medicine, he didn't need to learn their socialist philosophy to pass the boards.

One may surmise the government is no longer of the people but of the special interest groups, wealthy and those bent on the destruction of our country and way of life. While some regulations are needed the extent which our politicians have imposed them are not. The elitists have manipulated the system to subvert the constitution especially in the area of education. You have only look to the lack of historical knowledge our politician's exhibit to have a clear picture of this.

CHAPTER SIX

The Bureaucrats

The far left politicians are only part of the problem. The unelected far left bureaucrats present a greater threat as they exert considerable influence over our elected leaders. Perhaps that is why a synonym for bureaucrat is mandarin. They are the ones who collect and provide information to these elected officials involving important decisions. They are the epitome of the intellectual elite. Not all bureaucrats are this way. Many civil servants are fine hardworking people who attempt to do their best. Unfortunately, in government, there are many civil servants who work behind the scene to further a socialist agenda. Many of these bureaucrats attempt to weasel their way into steering policy decisions at all levels of government. A good example of this was after September 11, 2001.

We were attacked on our own soil. There was an outcry for a response. Some bureaucrats suggested we immediately strike Iraq as they were the most likely sponsors of this action. The Administration waited to get the facts which led to Afghanistan. Some Democrats and bureaucrats were pushing for a new government agency to handle these situations. Unknown to them, the President was conferring with key cabinet members who were using information compiled by bureaucrats. Finally, they had their feet held to the fire and were expected to do their job. Apparently over a period of approximately eight months the President and key members studied this information and used it to form the Office of Homeland Security, which later became a cabinet level department.

The bureaucrats went ballistic. They felt slighted because they were not part of this decision making process for such an important office. Over the years many of these bureaucrats have managed to gain more influence than they should in matters such as these. You may remember several of these bureaucrats resigning shortly after this. Our elected official, the President, did exactly what he was supposed to do. Have the unelected civil servants do their job by assimilating information and relaying this information to their boss, a cabinet member, who brought this information to the closed door planning sessions. This led to a fairly smooth development in establishing Homeland Security. The extreme left had a hard time with this because the bureaucracy failed to have a direct impact on the development of Homeland Security. Unfortunately, when Homeland Security became a cabinet level department the bureaucrats, once again, corrupted and manipulated the system, leading to an inept and impotent bureaucracy incapable of performing effectively!

My personal experience with one of these far left bureaucrats occurred when I was stationed at an US Air Force Base in the Southeast. I believe the behavior I witnessed of this particular civil servant is indicative of the few who connive their way into prominence.

I received my assignment to this base upon return from several extended overseas assignments. The commander of the organization was retiring within two months of my arrival. About a month after that, my boss, who worked for the commander relocated and was replaced by an officer who actually listened to subordinates. We had an excellent working relationship. Her responsibility was for the outpatient as well as inpatient areas. A well established chain of command was in place except for the inpatient areas.

I was one of the people in charge of the Emergency Medical Service (EMS). We developed and maintained operational control over all medical emergencies and ambulance response on base and the area immediately outside the gates. We had a great team of responders and care providers which made our job much easier. The unit consisted of all active duty personnel who were highly trained and motivated. After I was there a few months some of the personnel inquired if we needed more personnel or replacements for the people relocating to another base, the people assigned to the Same Day Surgery Unit were interested.

I asked my boss about this unit and she said it had only started a couple of months before I had arrived. She went on to say the unit was an experiment and the person in charge of the unit was a civilian who kept the unit's staff isolated from the rest of the medical facility's personnel.

Over the course of the next few months, some of the personnel assigned to this unit would approach me and ask if they could be assigned to the EMS. When asked why, most would reply they would like a change of pace. Since this unit was considered an inpatient unit I had very little interaction with the management and did not approach this civilian in charge about these personnel requesting reassignment. Usually, when you had most of the people assigned to a specific section requesting reassignment, it meant something was wrong.

As luck would have it, my boss finally decided to fill the position for the person in charge of the inpatient operations. I was asked to take the job which I accepted. I loved EMS but looked forward to a new challenge. I began the following Monday.

My first order of business was to evaluate each inpatient area. I decided to spend a few days orienting to each one starting on the top floor working down. It took several weeks to finally work my way down to the last unit which was the Same Day Surgery Unit. Along the way, I had many personnel asking why I was orienting on each unit. I told them I simply could not be in charge of all these units without knowing how they operate and knowing the abilities and motivation of all personnel assigned.

I needed to get a feel of these personnel to make assignment and reassignment decisions. All personnel I encountered on these units begged not to be reassigned to the Same Day Surgery Unit. This sent up red flags. I had a discussion with my boss before I was to orient on the Same Day Surgery Clinic. I explained what I had encountered and she said she had concerns about this unit but was told by the civilian in charge it was her unit and did not fall under our charge. I requested to continue with orienting and received permission.

I entered the unit on a bright sunny Monday and was greeted with a very cold shoulder by Ms. Karen the civil servant. I informed her I was there to become familiar with the unit and capabilities of the personnel. She said she knew all this information and didn't see why I needed to orient on "her" unit. I let her know I needed to become familiar with the personnel for future reassignments if necessary. She informed me she controlled all personnel of "her" unit and I would have to seek her permission to reassign anyone.

I could see this was going to be a battle. After the first day on this unit Ms. Karen became a little more relaxed. By the third day, I had kept such a low profile she acted as if I wasn't even there. Whenever I worked side by side with one of the personnel assigned I would ask subtle questions concerning how things were on the unit. It was unanimous, all personnel said that Ms. Karen was a power monger and things had become worse after arrival of the new commander and other high ranking personnel about the time I arrived. They said she had ambitions of climbing the ladder to the top and let them know they were her stepping stones. She made no effort to suppress of how much she loathed the military.

My last day on this unit, I decided to talk with Ms. Karen. I asked her what her plan was. We sat and talked, or rather she talked, for a couple of hours. She let me know she was on her way up and I had better get out of her way or she would squash me like a bug. I let her know she came behind active duty and although the ranking civilian on the unit, she too, had a chain of command.

After I left her office I discreetly asked the senior ranking enlisted and officer to meet in my office after their shift was over.

The officer and enlisted person and I sat down in my office to discuss how things got this way on this unit. I asked their opinion of Ms. Karen and both emphatically stated she is overstepping the mandate of the original establishment of this unit. They said her hire was for a finite period and her job description was very narrow in scope. They said after the current Commander signed in, this civil servant said she had a meeting with the commander and was put in complete control of the unit and personnel. They also stated she was always bragging about how she was going to work her way to the Pentagon and undermine military operations. According to them she did not believe in the U.S. Military and all funding should be put in social programs.

After talking with these two, I decided to investigate and informed my boss of the conversations and what I intended to do. She told me to do whatever discreetly and let her know what I found. I first checked with the Commander's secretary and asked for the contract and files for the Same Day Surgery Unit. She informed me the files had been taken when she wasn't there but thought they were maintained on the unit itself. She let me know in no uncertain terms she did not care for this person. I then went to the point of contact (POC) for civilian personnel issues assigned to the organization. I asked about any paperwork she would have only to be told it's kept in the Commander's office and the unit. As I was leaving she said the original and all amendments should be at the Civilian Personnel Office (CPO).

This was starting to not feel very discreet but I continued to keep a low profile anyway. The two ladies I talked with concerning this kept it to themselves as well, since they did not care for Ms. Karen. I talked with the head of the CPO who provided me copies of everything I asked for and more. I began researching the information as soon as I returned to my office.

It took two days but I found everything I needed. According to the contract the initial phase of the Same Day Surgery Unit had an end date of one year from the day it began and would not be extended. It went on to say the civilian who was "in charge" was actually hired as the accountant as this unit was supposed to be self sufficient by the funds it raised from insurance providers. Her contract hire was to be for the initial phase only and then the position would end. No amendments to either contract were found. Another point made in the contract was this position had no position of authority and was assigned to either me or my boss for supervision. The year had passed by about two months.

I briefed my boss and asked her if she wished for the civilian to be placed under me as dictated by the contract. She jumped on that. I then went to CPO and asked them who this person was assigned. They said Ms. Karen had brought them the paperwork for her assignment to the Commander about the time he arrived. I told them according to the contract she is to be assigned to me and to please change it immediately. The person in charge gladly made the change and back dated it and said Ms. Karen was due a performance evaluation that I would have to complete.

All this took place very quickly as I did not want her to get wind of what was about to happen. My boss and I went to the Commander and briefed him on what I had discovered and he breathed a sigh of relief. He said she was intimidating and had high aspirations and needed a lesson in humility. I asked him if we could keep this to the three of us until the Same Day Surgery staff meeting scheduled at 1600 hours Friday, which was a couple of days away. He and my boss thought that was a good idea. I spent the next couple of days coordinating and planning for what was to come.

Friday arrived and I was apprehensive and excited all day. I had a folder with all the documents I needed. At 1545 hours I made my way to the unit. I walked into the conference room and took a seat next to the ranking officer. The other staff members began to trickle in. At 1600 hours Ms. Karen came in and had an airman announce "atten-hut" for everyone to stand. I did not! This salutation is reserved for ranking officers when entering a room or meeting or such. The only civilian to be honored with this is the President of the United States. She glanced over at me and said, "Why are you not standing". I ignored her which made her furious. She must have figured something was up.

She told everyone to have a seat and then began to bring up items of interest. Part way through her dialogue I interrupted and asked the OIC what are the items she would like to bring up. Ms. Karen shouted, "This is my unit and you are not to interrupt me". I responded, "I was asking the Officer in Charge (OIC) if she had any items to discuss". She retaliated, "Get out of my meeting, I don't work for you". This is what I had anticipated would happen. In a calm voice I said, "Oh, yes you do." and handed her the paperwork assigning me as her supervisor. She audibly gasped. She knew the scam was over but she wasn't going without a fight.

She yelled, "Who do you think you are, by coming on my unit like this?" I told her lets go into the office and discuss this in private. She mistakenly took this as a sign of weakness instead of my attempt to minimize any more embarrassment she would endure by this public display. She yelled, "No! We are going to have this out right here so everyone knows who is in charge here."

I again suggested we discuss this in private. This emboldened her even more as she again shouted for me to leave "her unit". She began to rant about how some little insect was not going to stop her from getting to the Pentagon and how she was going to make me pay for my insolence.

I again suggested we discuss this in private. She shouted, "I'm in charge and we will discuss this right here". It was everything I could do to keep from raising my voice when I said, "That was your third strike and we will discuss it right here". This surprised her. I then told her of my investigation and how she had lied to the staff about being in charge of the unit. She began to protest when I told her I had affidavits from my boss and the Commander about how she erroneously led them to believe they had no control over her or the unit. I told her, "You are nothing but an accountant".

I handed her copies of the contract, personnel evaluation report and notice of termination of position. She yelled, "You can't do this, I don't work for you". I looked at my watch and noticed it was 1630 hours. I stated, "You worked for me until now. It is now time for you to leave and not come back". Outraged she said, "You can't do this to me". I turned and asked the ranking enlisted person to ask the two security police (SPs) outside the door to come in (that's what preplanning can do).

When the two SPs entered the room she told them to arrest me. I laughed along with the SPs and staff. I then handed her the document from the Base Commander and CPO stating she was banned from the base and blacklisted from any civilian position in the government. I asked the SPs to escort Ms. Karen out of the facility and off the installation. She said she had to get her personal things out of the office. The SPs and I walked with her to the office and along the way she said she would never give us the passwords to the computer information that would allow us access to all unit information and budgeting requirements.

She stopped dead in her tracks when she walked in the office. Behind her computer was one of our information systems technicians who I had come up the back stairs to "hack" the passwords for the unit. He turned as I entered and said, "I've got all her passwords and have access to all programs". Ms. Karen began to cry. I told her if she ever attempted to contact any personnel in this organization or apply for any position on this base, we would prosecute her to the fullest extent of the law. The SPs then confiscated her ID card and base pass and escorted her from the base.

This is a prime example of a bureaucrat out of control and one that is power hungry to the point of being absurd. While not all bureaucrats are like this, many are, and have manipulated themselves into very influential positions. I cannot emphasize the vast majority of civil servants are honest, hardworking Americans. The few who are not are the ones we must be alert to. I had the pleasure and opportunity to stop one before she weaseled into a position of influence. There are many more out there and can be found in all levels of government from local to federal.

The United States Constitution guarantees only one thing, DEFENSE of our freedoms. The primary line of defense is against invasion from outside our country. The military is the tool used for this defense. The elitists would have you believe otherwise. Since the 1950s circumvention and infiltration of our military appears to be a major goal of these "bleeding hearts". During my term of service I witnessed many people who attempted to undermine the whole system but that's for another book. To give you an idea of how the bureaucracy has attempted to achieve this take a look at troop strengths compared to civilian employees of the Department of Defense (DOD). In 1960, there were no conflicts or direct hostilities we were involved in. The active duty strength was approximately 2,480,438* and the DOD civilian employees numbered about 1,047,120*. The active duty personnel performed almost all housekeeping and outside maintenance on military installations along with pulling rotations in dining facilities to feed the troops. In 2001, active duty strength was 1,399,595* while civilians numbered 671,591*. Sounds equitable? On a percentage basis it comes to 43 ½ percent reduction for active duty and 36 percent for civilians. Most installations now have contracts for some housekeeping and outside maintenance and many of the tasks performed by active duty and civil servants as well. Many tasks active duty and civilian employees that were performed are now done by civilian contractors. The thought on this, it will free the troops up to focus on more complex training due to the high tech weapons systems we have today. I believe we all can agree this is a good idea. The problem is why has the DOD civilian employees not decreased substantially more. There is more than a 7 percent difference in the troop reduction. It should be the other way around. Active duty troops are there to fight if necessary. The civilians are primarily filling administrative positions. Don't get me wrong, we do need many of the civilian employees in the DOD. In my experience many of the middle management civilians spend more time justifying their positions than actually being productive. I believe we would be better served by converting many of these civilian positions to active duty positions. It can be done! We should focus on ones as in the preceding story so we can preserve those deserving and competent to keep their positions.

The reason many of these power hungry bureaucrats are very dangerous to the Republic of the United States is because they are not elected and can have significant influence on policy. We cannot afford to leave them unchecked.

CHAPTER SEVEN

Them or Us?

You ever notice when you're driving on the interstate, highway or street and look in your rearview mirror and see a police car pull behind you. Almost everyone immediately checks their speed, seatbelt and driving pattern. You tighten your grip on the steering wheel and become tense anticipating the flashing lights suddenly come on to pull you over. This is how most people would react, instead of thinking to yourself, "thank goodness, the police are here to ensure everyone's safety". This in itself shows we already live in a police state. When placed in this or a similar situation most people suddenly feel they are guilty of breaking some law. Most law enforcement personnel aren't looking to make your life miserable by giving you a ticket. Regrettably, some police do look forward to causing you problems. Some of these people have what I tend to call "them or us" syndrome.

Over the course of my military career I worked with several law enforcement organizations both in the United States and abroad. The last few years before leaving the military I encountered a disturbing trend among many law enforcement personnel. There seems to be a trend of the mentality by some in law enforcement of "them or us". I find this to be particularly unsettling as when I asked several of these law enforcement personnel for clarification on this, I was told "them" refers to all civilians and "us" refers to law enforcement. These officers feel if you are not one of "us" you have to be one of "them" and must not be trusted. You must remember the overwhelming majority of law enforcement personnel are good people who go the extra mile when performing their job. The minority of law enforcement are the ones who endanger the integrity of our system. They are rooted deep in the system and make it almost impossible to eliminate to clean the system.

You don't have to look far to see this trend. Take a look at some of the behind the scene footage from the Waco, Texas debacle in 1993. Some of the most disturbing scenes were not from the fire or from within the compound but outside the compound. Many of the law enforcement personnel bragged about being killing machines. Some went so far as to say these cult members deserved what they got. There are many discrepancies in the official version and what has been analyzed in the video. Do your own research and you will find many independent investigations which reveal some very disturbing behavior of some of the law enforcement personnel during the Waco catastrophe in which about 80 people died including 19 children. The members who survived this assault were fortunate enough to exit the side of the compound where the media could film them surrendering. Others who attempted to exit from the opposite side were not as lucky. The survivors' stories differ greatly from the government and much of the evidence corroborates the survivors' version.

Another well known situation was the Ruby Ridge incident where federal law enforcement personnel essentially attacked and killed several members of Randy Weaver's family. The government was found at fault and Mr. Weaver was awarded a settlement. No amount of money will bring his wife and son back due to excessive abuse of force by overzealous law enforcement.

Another lesser known incident occurred in 1985 in Philadelphia. This situation involved an alleged cult by the name of MOVE. When the police assaulted the residence in question the group barricaded the door. After a few days the overzealous police used an incendiary device to break through the roof. Sadly, 11 people were killed including 5 children and 61 homes were destroyed by fire.

These are serious incidents that made it to the media's attention due to the number of people involved. It could also be said this is a subtle attempt to label groups who are not part of the mainstream as cults or subversive or antigovernment. After all, the government seems to only want their official version of the story in view of the public. There are few survivors and their attempt to make their side of the story known has met great resistance. I believe the truth is somewhere in the middle.

I have three individuals in separate situations. Their names have been changed to protect them. Two of them experienced the abuse of police authority in New York City. The other experienced excessive police force in the suburbs of Tampa, Florida. While all three are guilty of certain crimes, the manner in which the police dealt with them is excessive.

The first case involved Joseph. He lived in a bad neighborhood with a crack addict for a mother. He was expected to support his family at the age of 14. Like most inner city kids, he had two strikes against him before he even had a chance. By the time he was fifteen, his mother had him making drug drops to support her habit and make money for food and rent. It didn't take long for Joseph to become involved in a gang. He saw what the drugs were doing to his family and he began looking for a way out.

His luck finally ran out and he was arrested for possession. The quantity was small so his sentence was only for a few months. When he was released from detention he went back to his neighborhood and was again drafted by the gangs. He managed to stay on the right side of the law except for parking tickets. He did accumulate several thousand dollars in parking fines.

One afternoon he was in his bedroom in his family's apartment. Suddenly, there was a pounding on the door and an inaudible yelling, then the door was smashed open with a battering ram. Several men rushed in with helmets, shields and batons. Thinking this may be a rival gang, he attempted to escape through a window but was stopped by men on the fire escape. He was thrown back into the apartment and beaten by these men who then identified themselves as police. They were there to serve Joseph with a warrant for unpaid parking violations. Since he attempted to run, they charged him with resisting arrest.

The police report states almost exactly what happened except that minimal force was used to subdue Joseph. Joseph managed to talk with a public defender, who, immediately brought in a photographer to take pictures of Joseph's injuries. It was obvious excessive force was used as his face is unrecognizable in the pictures. The dozen or so police who served the warrant maintain they used minimal force. Since when are a dozen police needed to serve a warrant for parking tickets?

Joseph's friend Miguel was less fortunate. He was busted for assault. During the course of the arrest he managed to get a hold of a baton and hit one of the arresting officers who then charged him with attempted murder. He was guilty and was sentenced to several years' incarceration. He served his time and was released. He told his parole officer (PO) he wanted to leave New York and live with his friend Joseph who had moved to another state. The PO told Miguel he would have to finish his probation before he would be allowed to leave.

Miguel quit hanging out with his old friends in his attempt to stay out of trouble. He found a job and tried to stay on the up and up. Then he encountered the "us" police. He was walking home from work one night when a patrol car stopped and questioned him. One of the officers recognized him and ordered him to empty his pockets. He had just cashed his pay check the day before and had the cash in his pocket. The police officer saw the cash and accused him of selling drugs. Miguel produced his pay stub but the police officer still accused him of selling drugs. He told Miguel since he was still on probation he would go back to jail for accusations of selling drugs. The police officer "confiscated" Miguel's

cash and told him not to let him catch
him dealing drugs again.

Miguel reported this to his PO who
accused him of making it up. A couple of
weeks later Miguel was again confronted
by the same police officers on his way
home from work. He was again accused of
selling drugs and his paycheck was
"confiscated" again. This time he had
hidden half of it in his shoe. When he
reported this to his PO he was once again
chastised and accused of not being
truthful. He asked the PO to help him
shorten his probation in order to leave
the city. The PO told him to deal with
it. Miguel is currently waiting to
complete his probation so he can move. He
has encountered the police officers
several times since and managed to hide
most of his money before they
"confiscate" it.

These two situations demonstrate how
corrupt some of our law enforcement
personnel are. Since these two had been
convicted in the past these officers
presumed guilt with no evidence to
support this guilt. In Miguel's case, the
officers stepped way over the line.
Unfortunately, Miguel cannot get justice
for being robbed as even the PO will not
give him the benefit of the doubt. Both
Joseph and Miguel are attempting to
straighten their lives out but in order
to do this they have to move to another
city.

The third situation involves a foolish sixteen year old in the suburbs of Tampa, Florida by the name of Francis. He is from a good family with a father who is a career military man. Francis made a mistake of "breaking in" someone's house and stealing and selling baseball cards. He was convicted when he was seventeen and part of his sentence was house arrest. His first parole officer was very fair and understanding and helpful in trying to get Francis on the right track.

Francis's parole officer (PO) was transferred and he was assigned another PO. This PO seemed to have a problem with everything Francis did. She would violate his probation for little things such as leaving school property when standing at the curb waiting for a ride home. A co-worker at the after school part time job he had, asked him to fill in for her on the weekend. He told her he couldn't because specifications in the house arrest were very strict in attending school and specific hours of working.

The cute little co-worker failed to show up for that shift and when questioned by the supervisor said Francis had agreed to cover her shift. The supervisor questioned Francis and decided to believe the young lady rather than him. The PO told Francis this again violated his probation.

Shortly after this, while his mother was at work and his father was on an extended temporary duty assignment. A so-called friend took advantage of a parent-free home and brought some alcohol over and they both became intoxicated. As luck would have it, Francis's PO stopped by the house to check on him. She considered this a major violation of his probation. She filed paperwork to the court indicating all the "violations" of his probation. There is no question this now 17 year old was acting as many other 17 year olds act which doesn't justify this behavior. It's also no reason to try and send him to jail for a year.

Francis's father had been on temporary military assignment for several months and still had several months left before returning home. Francis's mother had to carry the burden alone as is the case in many military families. One morning, at approximately 2:00 AM she was startled awake by a pounding at the front door. On her way to the see who it was at the front door, she noticed shadows in the backyard and someone appearing to gain access at the back door. She looked through the sidelight of the front door and saw several men standing there and a sheriff's patrol car with its lights flashing at the curb. She opened the door only to have several flashlights shined in her face.

One of the men asked if Francis was there as they wanted to question him. She stated he was and they barged in and went to his bedroom where they woke him and placed handcuffs on him. If it weren't for the cruiser with its strobe lights on in the front neither Francis nor his mother would have known these were law enforcement personnel. When they escorted Francis outside his mother followed and asked what was going on.

The deputy told her Francis was being arrested for violating his probation. While the deputy was talking with his mother she noticed there were several more cruisers and a S.W.A.T. vehicle. The shadow in the backyard was S.W.A.T. personnel preparing for an assault to serve a warrant for a non-violent probation violation. When asked why this warrant served during normal daylight hours the deputy replied, "We like to use the element of surprise."

On further investigation it was found when someone like this violates probation a summons is issued for the individual to appear in court. Only if the individual fails to appear in court will a warrant for arrest be issued. This clearly did not happen in this case.

You have to ask, why was an all out tactical assault planned in this case? Was it an intimidation tactic? Could it be a show of force to frighten others?

Who really knows? One thing is certain. Francis's father was away performing military duty. Knowing him the way I do, if he were home when this assault occurred, he would have taken the appropriate action of defending his home.

If he saw the shadowy figures in the back attempting to gain access he would have armed himself and dialed 911 to report someone attempting to break in. If 911 personnel were slow to inform him of what was going on, he surely would have opened fire. He would have every right to do so as the law enforcement failed to identify who they were and the measures used were completely inappropriate. This arrest tactic is the same used by the Gestapo in Nazi Germany, the KGB in the former USSR, and secret police of Saddam Hussein's Iraq among numerous other police states.

We have incidents occurring almost everyday here in this country. June 19, 2004 in Mequon, Wisconsin, a 20 year old young man* died of suffocation while in police custody. Everyone is in agreement the police did not intentionally cause this young man's suffocation. But let's look to the facts leading up to this incident. There supposedly was a call of a gas "drive-off" of which the police responded. A "drive-off is when someone fills their vehicle with gas at a station and then drives off without paying. For some reason the police mistakenly pulled over the vehicle in which this young man was a passenger. According to conflicting reports a "pipe" (the kind you smoke) was near where this young man was sitting. The police assumed this was drug paraphernalia and ordered the occupants out of the car. The video showed the police throwing this young man to the ground face down causing him to get a mouthful of grass. Once the man was handcuffed the police helped him to his feet and he began spitting the grass out of his mouth. I seem to remember several eye witnesses being interviewed about this event to corroborate this. For some reason the police took this to mean he was spitting at them and one of them retrieved a hood to place over this man's head. Unfortunately, a mistake was made and a hazardous material hood was placed over his head. This hood does not allow you to breathe fresh air unless a mouthpiece is placed in the mouth of the person wearing the hood. On the audio on the police video you can hear the man say he had asthma and could not breathe. One officer, who reportedly had training as an emergency medical technician (EMT) said, "If you can talk, you can breathe". Regrettably, the prisoner was not reevaluated until it was too late. While enroute to the police station action taken by the police officers should have been different. This is not the issue. Several questions arise concerning the whole situation. Once the police pulled the suspected "drive-off" over was the license plates checked for verification? Why did the police apparently "target" this young man when they supposedly saw a pipe in the car? Witnesses saw the young man spitting to get the grass out of his mouth, why could the police not determine this was what the man was doing instead of trying to spit at them? Perhaps, overzealous officers misinterpreted the situation. This is one of many situations of possible excessive force. This was a high profile case broadcast on national news.

There are numerous cases of abuses by law enforcement personnel. Another high profile case was concerning Elian Gonzales*. This case involved a young boy taken by his mother from his father after the court awarded him custody. This family lived in Cuba at the time. The mother and her current boyfriend attempted to escape to the United States by boat. The mother and boyfriend drowned in the attempt but Elian survived and was rescued by U.S. personnel. The child was placed with relatives in Miami while the father went to the courts to regain custody of his son. The family in Miami refused to let Elian go and there was a stand-off. Instead of properly negotiating with these people to return Elian to his father, the Attorney General, Janet Reno, apparently ordered an armed assault team to go in the house and take Elian by force. Although, no one in the house was thought to be armed the team went in with guns drawn and force we don't even see in Iraq. The top law enforcement person exhibited a habit of ordering or condoning excessive force throughout her reign not only as the U.S. Attorney General but the Florida AG as well. While I strongly believe Elian should have been returned to his father in Cuba, the method used is inexcusable.

Here's one from Al Gore's state of Tennessee. In January 2003, a family was on their way home from Nashville to South Carolina*. When leaving a gas station the father forgot his wallet on the roof of his car. Motorists saw his money fly when he took off and called police. In the video, released by the Tennessee Hwy Patrol (THP), officers are heard ordering the family, one by one, to get out of their car with their hands up. The father and his wife, and 17-year-old son were ordered onto their knees and handcuffed. "What did I do?" the father asks the officers. "Sir, inside information is that you were involved in some type of robbery in Davidson County," the unidentified officer says. The man and his wife protest in amazement, telling the officers that they are from South Carolina and that their mother and father-in-law are traveling in another car alongside them. As they knelt, handcuffed, they pleaded with officers to close the doors of their car so their two dogs would not escape, but the officers did not heed them. The Wife is seen on the tape looking up at an officer, telling him slowly, "That dog is not mean. He won't hurt you." Her husband says, "I got a dog in the car. I don't want him to jump out." The tape then shows a medium-size brown dog romping on the shoulder of the Interstate, its tail wagging. As the family yells, the dog, first heads away from the road, then quickly circles back toward the family. An officer in a blue uniform aims his shotgun at the dog and fires at its head, killing it immediately. For several moments, all that is audible are shrieks as the family reacts to the shooting. The father even stands up, but officers pull him back down. "Y'all shot my dog! Y'all shot my dog!" He cries. "Oh my God! God Almighty!" "You shot my dog!" screams his wife, distraught and still handcuffed. "Why'd you kill our dog?" "Jesus, tell me, why did y'all shoot my dog?" He says.

The officers bring him to the patrol car, and the family calms down, but still they ask the officers for an explanation. One of them says Patton was "going after" the officer. "No he wasn't, man," He says. "Y'all didn't have to kill the dog like that."

The family describes the dog as playful and gentle, "like Scooby-Doo" and may have simply gone after the beam of the flashlight as he often did at home, when the 17 year old and the dog would play.

Is this how police react to an unconfirmed report of a crime? Do you know what would happen if you shot a family pet in your neighborhood if you thought it was "going after" you? Are these officers even trained to appraise a possible dangerous situation? These actions are typical in the "them or us" mentality. Since this family wasn't one of us they had to be one of them and dealt with appropriately.

Remember up until 20 or so years ago, when almost all law enforcement personnel wore a distinctly identifiable uniform? Most local police wore a crisp blue uniform and county deputies wore various crisp uniforms. Of course, undercover officers wore the appropriate attire to better perform their job. Over the course of the last 2 decades the uniforms in most localities seem to have deteriorated into combat style uniforms from head to toe. Now we see what some call "jack booted thugs" due to their attire. The justification for these officers to wear hoods is to "protect" their identities. This may be true in covert operations but not in police work. This rationalization is the same that has been used by the Gestapo in Nazi Germany, the former Soviet secret police, Saddam's Republican Guard and various special police in countries with dictatorships. The next time you're pulled over by a police officer look and see if they're dressed as a police officer or as a "jack booted thug"!

Don't get me wrong, I believe the vast majority of law enforcement officers are doing a great job. Considering the obstacles they faced in dealing with drugs, violent crime and corruption it's understandable errors will be made. The problem is not with these people but with the ones who consider all other citizens as "them". All it takes is a few to muddy the reputation of the rest. Unfortunately, more and more seem to be separating the citizenry especially those law enforcement personnel at higher levels of government.

CHAPTER EIGHT

Liberal Mentality
And
Rewards

Let me start by saying this is not a Democrat or Republican mentality. As I stated previously, the overwhelming majority of Americans are moderate and the true term liberal or conservative does not apply. Moderate would be a more appropriate description. When I write liberal I intend its meaning to reflect the elitist mentality. There are many elitists who claim to be Republican especially at the lower levels of government. Republicans are more defined at the federal level but the local levels have many "sheep in wolves clothing". Check their proposals and voting records and you will see.

As you've heard before what the liberals can't control they attempt to destroy. One of the most important is the sanctity of life. While many of these elitists are against capital punishment they whole-heartedly support fetal genocide through abortion. These people think a fetus is not a human being because they have not been born yet. Not only are abortions performed in the first two trimesters of pregnancy but the third as well. Indisputable fact is the third trimester produces a viable fetus that can survive outside the womb. Some would argue differently but check the facts. Look at the example of the smallest baby* born just last year. Normal gestation is about 40 weeks. Complications arose in this pregnancy and a caesarean section was performed and delivered the 8.6 ounce little girl. Some would say this is an exception. Well her twin sister weighed a whopping 1 pound 4 ounces. This is significant because this delivery was in the last part of the second trimester. Another baby* weighing 11 ounces at 23 weeks gestation was born in New Jersey in 2003. There are cases such as these all over the world. Faced with these facts, how can anyone claim a fetus is not a human being? If you take the aborted fetus and test the tissue from the remains what DNA will you find? The elitists would have you believe the DNA is not relevant. That would be true if the DNA was that of a dog, pig, goat or some other animal. The DNA is undeniably that of a human being. Although if you're dealing with some animal rights activists they would disagree and believe the DNA is irrelevant as animals should be treated as humans.

A good example of how distorted some elitists or bleeding hearts beliefs are look to the leader in clouding this issue of Boulder, Colorado*. Animal rights groups, such as In Defense of Animals

(IDA), advocates animals are more than personal property. Their goal is to shift legal status of animals from property to personhood. To do this they are convincing many cities to replace "owner" with "guardian". Many cities have deceptively been led to believe this is a low cost, symbolic gesture that which will lead to the pet owners to provide better care for their pets. West Hollywood, Berkeley, California and the General Assembly of Rhode Island essentially followed suit. The American Veterinarian Medical Association sponsored a task force* to evaluate the change from owner to guardian. The task force investigated the legal ramifications and determined a myriad of problems with this change.

To begin you have to understand the definition of the two. Ownership is a collection of rights to use and enjoy property. Guardianship is a legal arrangement under which one person has the legal right and duty to care for another. The one cared for is considered a ward. Existing laws in all states view domestic and companion animals as property. The associated rights of ownership include the right to control, handle and sell property. When consulting a veterinarian for care of the animal the owner has the right to accept or reject medical treatment. Cruelty and humane treatment are covered under other laws within the state. With guardianship, the interest of the ward is the overriding concern and all decisions are made in the ward's best interest. The problem is, with guardianship any interested person can petition the court for a change in guardianship, and the court can grant the change. As with other issues you will not see much of a change for the first few years then the lawsuits will start.

Do you keep your dog outside on a chain? Maybe your dog's house or kennel isn't heated or air conditioned. If you have horses and you have them on a pasture or clean their stall every 2 weeks instead of weekly. These are instances where some bleeding heart elitists can petition the court for guardianship and if adjudicated against you, your pet can be removed and placed with the petitioner, and you will not be compensated. You most likely will incur the legal costs of the petitioner.

Any faithful Christian understands we are not to misuse, abuse or neglect animals but these people are going to far. Genesis 1:26 — "…and let them have dominion over the fish of the sea, and over the fowl of the air, and over the cattle, and over all the earth, and over every creeping thing that creepeth upon the earth". This quote appears to be lost on many. This pervasive mentality seems to have originated in England. My family and I lived about 2 hours north of London for 3 ½ years. I can safely say the predominant mentality there is not looking out for humans. I have 2 stories about our time in England which I'll blend together.

We lived there in the mid 1980s. It was an unusually bright sunny but cold day. The sun shining, in itself, was unusual. My wife and I decided to travel to downtown Ipswich to go Christmas shopping at the local Woolworth. The Woolworth was one of the few department stores in the area and was supplied with a decent amount of goods. We had 4 children at the time, the oldest about 9 years old and the youngest about 1 ½ years old. We parked around the corner and walked down the street passing prams (baby carriages) bumped up against one another in a line all the way past the entrance to Woolworth. We did not pay much attention to this as it was not an unusual sight. We entered the store and my wife went shopping in the clothing department. I took the kids to the toy department to spy what they liked so I could come back later and purchase it for Christmas. The massive toy department was downstairs and was full of people. My hyperactive kids were playing with everything, but I managed to keep them under control. Of course, the Brits were giving us odd and very disapproving looks but what's new. After awhile, my wife found us and we slowly made our way to the stairs. Along the way I asked my wife if she noticed anything out of the ordinary. She started looking around and when we approached the top of the stairs, she said she didn't notice any young children in the toy department. She was right, the only kids there were about 10 years old and up and adults. Our kids were the only young ones there. We approached the front doors and I told my wife to look in the prams on the way back to the car. We looked in each pram we passed, bundled in each one was a child ranging from infant to way past toddler. Although they were bundled up to keep warm they were all unattended. This was a big cultural difference between America and Great Britain. I asked several co-workers about this and was told this is how it has always been.

A few weeks later, we had a babysitter care for our kids so my wife and I could go back to Woolworth and buy Christmas presents. It was late in the day and not many people were out shopping compared to the other day we went. We reached the front door and noticed a medium sized terrier being tied by the owner to the lamp post in front of the store. We went in and again noticed an absence of small children. This time we did notice that many people had their leashed dogs with them. Some of the animals walked with their owners while others were carried. We gathered the items we wished to purchase and went to the checkout and noticed the gentleman behind us was the one who had tied his pet to the lamp post outside. We managed to gather our packages about the same time the gentleman completed his checkout. We pushed through the doors and came face to face with a police officer. He inquired if the animal tied to the post was ours. The gentlemen stepped forward and said it was his and he had only tied it there for a moment. The man was arrested for the charge of animal neglect and the dog was taken away by animal control officers. In England it appeared pets receive greater protection than children. This sick mentality has now reached our shores. The elitists love this distortion because it causes more confusion within our society leading to a greater loss of personal control and clouds the perception as to right and wrong.

This confusion is evident in the area of stem cell research. The ones in support of fetal stem cell research are either the elitist or has been mislead as to the facts. The most important fact is fetal stem cells are the direct result of loss of a life. Adult stem cells have proven to be more effective in research. First, you need to understand exactly what stem cells are.

Adult stem cells are undifferentiated cells found among differentiated cells of a specific tissue and are mostly multi-potent cells. They are already being used in treatments for over one hundred diseases and conditions. They are more

130

accurately called *somatic* stem cells, because they need not come from adults but can also come from children or umbilical cords.

Embryonic stem cells are cultured cells obtained from the inner mass cells of a blastocyst. Embryonic stem cell research is still in the basic research phase. Research with embryonic stem cells derived from humans is controversial because, in order to start a stem cell 'line' or lineage, it requires the destruction of a blastocyst (an embryo that has not yet grown beyond 150 cells). Scientists have been researching fetal stem cells almost as long as adult stem cells.

The elitists would have you believe the destruction of embryos will provide greater use of stem cells. The fact is although fetal stem cells have been experimented with almost as long as adult stem cells not one practical application has been discovered. For years we've heard how close the scientists are in a "breakthrough" using fetal stem cells. During this time hundreds, thousands and maybe more fetuses have been murdered.

On the other side using adult stem cells have produced amazing successes. Breakthrough treatment in paralysis due to spinal cord injuries, Parkinson's disease and numerous other illnesses are the result of adult stem cells. A team of

Korean researchers reported on November 25, 2004, that they had transplanted multi-potent adult stem cells from umbilical cord blood to a patient suffering from a spinal cord injury and she can now walk on her own, with difficulty. The patient could not even stand up for the last 19 years. That, is progress, not the empty promise of an "almost breakthrough" we've been hearing for years.

Misleading the public is what these elitists seem to do best. They don't want to deal in facts just emotion. They prey on the emotions of those they wish to influence. These radicals have infiltrated areas of influence especially our higher schools of learning. We see these professors who promote the socialist ideology and punish students who exhibit individualism and free thought. One professor calls Christians "stupid" while another calls for students to take up arms and overthrow the government. Is this what you want your college age children exposed to? Science appears to have evolved into a process to disprove God's existence. This seems to further the agenda of the extremists. Not all scientists and professors exhibit this left wing flawed philosophy but far more do. Many professors and scientists who reflect the majority of our beliefs keep a low profile for fear of reprisal. This reminds me of a story a friend told me. He seemed to think it was factual but I can't attest that it is.

A group of scientists were working on the "big bang" theory of how the universe began. They took all the available data and charted the constellations. They used discoveries and charts from several hundred years ago and compared them to the current mappings. They used computer simulations to work through the calculations. They determined after its initial appearance, the universe apparently inflated (the "Big Bang"), expanded and cooled, going from very, very small and very, very hot, to the size and temperature of our current universe. It continues to expand and cool to this day and we are inside of it. Creatures living on a unique planet, circling a beautiful star clustered together with several hundred billion other stars in a galaxy soaring through the cosmos, all of which is inside of an expanding universe that began as an infinitesimal singularity which appeared out of nowhere for reasons unknown. This is the Big Bang theory. These scientists confirmed this theory as they found galaxies appear to be moving away from us at speeds proportional to their distance. This is called "Hubble's Law," named after Edwin Hubble (1889-1953) who discovered this phenomenon in 1929. This observation supports the expansion of the universe and suggests that it was once compacted. Now the big question is how and why, did this occur! Nothing existed prior to the Big Bang so how can something come from nothing? One scientist, a devout Christian, claimed this proves the existence of God. The other scientists scoffed at him and chastised him for his faith. They said it was ridiculous to even suggest nothing was there and then his so-called God snapped his non-existent fingers and suddenly the Big Bang happened. They felt something had to exist prior to the Big Bang. These scientists continued to study this dilemma.

The day of this criticism the Christian went home and closed off one room in his house and began working on an accurate model of the solar system. Everyday he would go to work and study with his colleagues but would return home and work on his model. He kept this a secret from them while he worked on this project privately. It took over a year to complete. He had the complete solar system suspended to scale in this room. He decided to invite his fellow scientists over for dinner to show them this model. They arrived for dinner and sat in the living room while the host's wife prepared dinner. He asked if his fellow scientists would like to see something extraordinary. They all said yes. He asked them to follow him as he led them to the room. He opened the door to the room where the model was. The room was dark and he asked them to step in the room no more than 2 feet from the door. Once they were all in he turned the light on. They all let out an audible gasp. They couldn't believe it. They gazed upon the model in disbelief. One asked how did he manage to get this much detail? Another asked how long did this take to complete? The chief scientist asked, "How in the world did he do this?" The Christian scientist said, "You know, it's a funny thing. One day I came in the room and opened the window. When I turned around, it was just there". The other scientists said, "That's absolutely ridiculous and impossible". He replied, "How can it be ridiculous and impossible if that's the same theory you have of the origin of the universe?"

You see this is how the elitists think. If they can't touch, see or feel, it cannot be real. These people try and convince others to believe this way but they refuse to totally convince themselves. They are the ones you see going to church every Sunday but act like God doesn't exist Monday through Saturday. Their personal and business dealings are virtually absent of anything relating to God. They're the ones who preach the separation of Church and state because they don't want God's influence in government. Some of these people even form organizations and profess to be Christians and even ministers but doesn't want religion anywhere in government. I call these people Pseudo-Christians. In their heart they don't believe God exists but they want to keep their toe in the door just in case. I guess they feel God is so forgiving that if they keep a toe in the door they won't suffer when they die. All true Christians know all debts must be paid either now or later.

This leads to the mentality of trying to influence the direction of our country. This is especially true in resistance to appointment of judicial nominees with traditional values and views. The elitists who embrace the Pseudo-Christian mentality are very transparent with this issue. We'll look at only one situation. President Bush nominated Priscilla Owen to the federal bench and was blocked by these socialists for several years before finally receiving a vote. She was confirmed 56-43. The confirmation numbers alone speak volumes about these obstructionists. The far left accuse Judge Owen of judicial activism. One of their main instances is her dissent concerning parental notification of a minor when receiving an abortion. The facts are clear as the law states the minor must meet certain requirements in order to qualify for a "bypass" order from the court. Judge Owen adhered to strict interpretations of the law as it is written and was correct in her dissent and opposition to other members of the court. She made her decision without any political motivation and is correct in reading the law this way. Perhaps some of the other judges on this court were looking ahead from a political standpoint. In her view the minor in this case did not present adequate evidence to warrant a "bypass" order. So it boils down to this. When a judge makes a judgment in favor of parental rights or family values the elitists consider it activism. This comes from people who want to restrict parental rights, supply murder (abortion) on demand, repeal the death penalty in all cases and legalize homosexual marriage. It appears traditional values, which many have existed for thousands of years, are taboo while these modern philosophies and perversions are rammed down our throats.

Another good example of how these elitists think is the President's nomination of John Bolton to represent the United States in the United Nations. What better way to facilitate change in the UN than for someone who knows the UN for what it is. He may be blunt and lacks tact but that is what is needed for us at this juncture. The far left prefer the status quo. They do not want to rock the boat or for the UN to change course. Why is that? Could it be possible the UN has been working to achieve the socialist agenda in our country! Research Agenda 21 if you truly would like the answer to this!

Look at what's going on in your local community to get a glimpse of what these socialists have in mind for you. Take a look at the leash law in your community. We've found some which will allow you to be cited if your dog is in your yard without a fence. What if your child is throwing a Frisbee for your dog to catch? What about the electronic fence many people now have? According to some of these leash laws, you can be cited. What about rabies vaccine? Do you think government officials should be allowed to perform door to door searches for rabies vaccinations? This is a blatant violation of our 4th Amendment rights. The following is my experience when our county decided to trample the constitution.

In January 2005, some politicians made a decision that the rabies control veterinarian could make house to house searches for rabies certificates for dogs*. I don't object to verification of rabies vaccine when living in a neighborhood or your pets are exposed to the public. We have a small farm and our dogs are isolated and are not exposed to other dogs. We live at the end of a dead end road and many people especially those in one of the affluent developments just down the road dump their unwanted pets at the end of our road. At first we would take the dogs to the County Humane Society. We took the third batch of puppies from an unwanted pet, which was dumped, and the volunteer was crying when she came out to the truck to get them. She said although they were puppies they would be euthanized as soon as we drove away. These puppies were brought back home. Although I have a realistic view of animals I do not believe in killing them for no reason. We have built a kennel out of concrete blocks, concrete floor and chain link fence with 4 separate cages with runs which houses most of the dogs. We have around 15 dogs at any given time. All have their rabies shots and I immunize them for other requirements myself.

It was a couple of months into this illegal search when I was walking back to the house from the barn when I saw my wife talking with a man driving a pickup with government license plates. When I walked up my wife introduced him as the official who was to check our dogs rabies certificates. My wife asked where they were and she would go get them. This gave me a chance to talk with this gentleman. I told him my views and my hostility was not directed at him but the illegal action the government was taking in this matter. I told him it was a bogus excuse and this was the county government attempt to try and exert control over us. He attempted to assure me it wasn't bogus and it was mandated by the state. I told him I could prove it was. He asked, "How?" I asked him why cats rabies vaccines were not being checked. He said cats were not as susceptible as dogs were. I asked, "What about horses?" since they were a high risk group as well. I told him we didn't vaccinate our horses against rabies. He said he grew up on a dairy farm and they vaccinated their horses against rabies. I then told him cows, goats and sheep were at a higher risk than dogs, why were they not being required rabies vaccinations? He said he didn't have an answer for me. About that time my wife came up with the certificates and tags. He reviewed the certificates and tags and then began walking toward the kennel. I asked him, "Where are you headed?" He said he was going down to the kennel. I said, "Oh, no you're not!" He turned and apparently saw I was serious. After a moment he told us he could see we were trying to take care of the dogs and we obviously had the documents in order. He then returned to his truck and left without further incident.

Some of you may think my actions were inappropriate. They are not! I am a strict constitutionalist and take great exception to any government entity that has a total disregard for the US and State Constitution. The area I live contain many people with the same views as I and many are veterans who've sacrificed much for this country. Because of this, the elitists who've migrated to our county are using every attempt to exert control over those freedom loving citizens. If this were not true, why did heavily populated areas in other parts of the county not have someone go around and check the vaccination certificates? Not to mention, if this was mandated by the state why were the other surrounding counties not experiencing anyone making house to house searches?

The collective (socialist) system of rewards can be seen throughout the country. In simple terms the elitist believe the group is more important than the individual. This is one of the basis for atheism. As Norman Mailer said, "The function of socialism is to raise suffering to a higher level." Many institutions, such as state welfare systems, job training programs, homeless shelters, and charitable organizations thrive by maintaining sizeable constituencies from the ranks of the unemployed and impoverished. This leads to them becoming an indispensable part of the system enhancing the institutionalized control of people. Examples of the collective domination of individuals are willing slaves, men and women who submit to remain dependent on established authorities for their livelihoods will remain submissive enough to pose no threat to the ruling order.

How popular is the "Park and Ride" program in your area? This has been advertised as energy conscious and aid in decreasing traffic congestion. Combine this mentality with some cities which have a "car pool" lane. Try driving in one of these lanes on your way to work one morning. Surely, you can see the reward for submitting to the collective will of the ruling elite? I find it interesting these elitists haven't given up their chauffeurs, gas guzzling luxury vehicles, commuter planes or other personal transportation. Of course not, the rules apply to everyone else, not them. Just ask Ted Kennedy.

Another important sign to show how collectivism is rewarded is how the government imposes property tax. Homeowners must pay but apartment dwellers do not. The argument is the owners of the apartments collect enough rent they pay the property tax for each family occupying an apartment. Sounds good but this is not quiet true. While the apartment owners pay property taxes it equates to much less than home owners in the same area.

I know of a family that lived in a roomy apartment in a very nice area. Rent was around five hundred fifty dollars a month for a good sized four bedroom apartment. They found a house in the very same area that suited their needs well. The house itself was slightly larger than the apartment but it had a garage. The monthly house payment is about seven hundred-fifty dollars. On top of that, property tax is approximately nine hundred dollars a year. According to the county tax assessor's website the breakdown for the individual apartment property tax comes to approximately three hundred dollars.

According to my itemized tax bill approximately seventy-five percent of property taxes collected go for education. Essentially the apartment dweller is paying less per month for occupancy but there is no extra payment of taxes as they are paid by the apartment owner. So, you see, by forgoing ownership of a house you are rewarded by paying considerably less or virtually not at all for your children's education. The tax incentive for owning your own home is much less than the difference in payments. Granted, if you keep the house long enough you may get a return on your investment unless the economy in your area tanks. If you don't think this can happen ask some military families who bought houses in Alaska in the late 1970s and early 1980s. Many ended up with houses worth almost one hundred thousand dollars less than what was owed on their homes.

Hopefully you are getting a clear picture of the elitist philosophies and the attempts to reward people who submit to the collective will of the ruling elite. This attitude is so much more pervasive in the local levels of government that much of it escapes our radar. We seem to be so much more attentive of actions at the national level that we seem to forget local governments have a far greater impact on our daily lives. Since many of the local media outlets are greatly influenced by the ruling elite we seldom get a straight story unless we do the investigating ourselves. These elitists believe the rules do not apply to them therefore equality before the law should be demolished to make place this privileged ruling class, who want to control the economy for its own interest and fat pockets. This is humiliating and hypocritical. History has proven concentration of power leads to atrocities. Taxation ties everyone's hands causing half of their time being dedicated to the state to pay these taxes. The wars on drugs, terrorism, poverty and crime all give government a blank check on our rights, and give increased powers to the police.

Philip D. Reed said it best with, "A PRIMER OF AMERICAN SELF-GOVERNMENT I. Understand, honor and preserve the Constitution of the United States. 2. Keep forever separate and distinct the legislative, executive and judicial functions of government. 3. Remember that government belongs to the people, is inherently inefficient, and that its activities should be limited to those which government alone can perform. 4. Be vigilant for freedom of speech, freedom of worship, and freedom of action. 5. Cherish the system of Free Enterprise which made America great. 6. Respect

thrift and economy, and beware of debt.
7. Above all, let us be scrupulous in
keeping our word and in respecting the
rights of others."

CHAPTER NINE

Oligarchy
Ruling From the Bench

Over the past forty years the elitists have been quietly "stacking the deck" in their favor by appointments to the courts. This has occurred at all levels of the judiciary. The result is the ruling elite have gained control of decision making which impacts every aspect of our lives. This handful of elitists, reflect an oligarchy. An oligarchy is "a small group of people who together govern a nation or control an organization, often for their own purposes". How very evident in the liberal leaning Supreme Court. There have been many rulings that actually violate the U.S. Constitution, yet, these activists judges are getting away with it. Why? The movers and shakers of the far left agenda have been discreetly "seeding" our courts in attempts to control and/or destroy individual rights in this country. Let's take a look at some of these unconstitutional rulings.

Take the decision of the U.S. Supreme Court ROE v. WADE, 410 U.S. 113 (1973)

...3. State criminal abortion laws, like those involved here, that except from criminality only a life-saving procedure on the mother's behalf without regard to the stage of her pregnancy and other interests involved violate the Due Process Clause of the Fourteenth Amendment, **which protects against state action the right to privacy,** including a woman's qualified right to terminate her pregnancy. Though the State cannot override that right, it has legitimate interests in protecting both the pregnant woman's health and the potentiality of human life, each of which interests grows and reaches a "compelling" point at various stages of the woman's approach to term.Pp.147-164

Notice the ruling states a right to privacy. No where in the U.S. Constitution does it state the destruction of a fetus is a privacy matter. The elitists would have you believe it does. U.S. Constitution Amendment XIV Section 1 states, "All persons born or naturalized... nor shall any State deprive any person of life, liberty, or property, without due process of law..."! Elitist lawyers would have you believe abortion falls under what they call the doctrine of "Substantive Due Process." When the doctrine of substantive due process was initially announced, it was limited in this way, the Court said it embraces only those liberties that are fundamental to a democratic society and rooted in the traditions of the American people.

In March 2005, a speech to the Woodrow Wilson International Center Justice on Constitutional Interpretation, Supreme Court Justice Antonin Scalia states, "...that limitation is eliminated. Within the last 20 years, we have found to be covered by due process the right to abortion, which was so little rooted in the traditions of the American people that it was criminal for 200 years; the right to homosexual sodomy, which was so little rooted in the traditions of the American people that it was criminal for 200 years. So it is literally true, and I don't think this is an exaggeration, that the Court has essentially liberated itself from the text of the Constitution, from the text and even from the traditions of the American people. It is up to the Court to say what is covered by substantive due process. In a nutshell he said that the Constitution is not supposed to be "interpreted." It is supposed to mean what the document SAID it meant when written in 1787."

The Oligarchy of the Supreme Court did not uphold the U.S. Constitution but actually used a creative manipulation for an erroneous interpretation to fit a law to conform to the elitist mentality that was prevalent at the time this decision was made.

In addition to the above facts I can prove from a secular point abortion is UNCONSTITUTIONAL! Before the Articles of the U.S. Constitution the first paragraph states,

> "We the People of the United States, in Order to form a more perfect Union, establish Justice, insure domestic Tranquility, provide for the common Defence, promote the general Welfare, and secure the Blessings of Liberty to ourselves and our **Posterity**, do ordain and establish this Constitution for the United States of America."

The definition of posterity (before the revisionists distorted the dictionaries and history books) is "future generations, the **unborn**". This proves an unborn fetus has the right to have the government "...provide for the common **Defence**, promote the general **Welfare**, and secure the **Blessings of Liberty...**"! Not only does the U.S. Constitution affirm the right to life but essentially is the basis for the Declaration of Independence, "We hold these truths to be self-evident, that all men are created equal, that they are endowed by their Creator with certain unalienable Rights, that among these are **Life**, Liberty and the pursuit of Happiness..."! This is the non-religious fact to support pro-life.

Apparently, the Supreme Court failed to actually read the Constitution and Declaration of Independence for what it actually states. Once again, no one has been able to show me where the taking of the life of a fetus is a privacy issue or even a "substantive due process" in the Constitution. If these pro-abortion people are so bent on the "privacy" issue, why is there no outcry about people being told, along with the enforcement of wearing of a seatbelt, yet, considered not to violate your privacy*. The elitists provide one argument as wearing a seatbelt may prevent you from becoming injured or killed. (Don't you think that's your decision?) These people somehow overlook the fact an abortion does kill at least one victim and endangers another (mother) every time one is performed.

For some reason there seems to be a belief that as long as the cord is attached to the baby, even at term, that an abortion can still be performed. We see this occurring in late term abortions apparently on a routine basis. Let's call it what it is, an abortion is the termination of an unwanted life. There have been several cases of mothers who've terminated the lives of their children* and they have been tried and put in jail or a psychiatric facility.

Why did the lawyers not use the most plausible excuse? Based on judges making up laws as they go I believe a case can be made for the most compelling argument. It's really very simple. The murders of these children are no more than, what I call, "post-birth abortion". Think about the wide ranging effects that can have on future murders. Think about the applications! You know the guy in your neighborhood everyone dislikes and has no use for. He never cuts his grass, trims his hedges, paints his house, keeps his privacy fence in good repair and lets his dog run loose terrorizing the neighborhood. This guy, much like the aborted fetus, is unwanted in your neighborhood. Attempts to make him move are unsuccessful. Sure, just like the unwanted fetus, he may have family somewhere that may want him or another neighborhood that would welcome him but he just won't go away on his on. You and some other neighbors have had enough so, one day, you take it upon yourselves to brutally slice him to pieces resulting in his death. The police investigation reveals the fact the guy was unwanted and served no useful purpose for the greater good of the neighborhood. You're arrested though and charged with murder. Shouldn't your defense be the obvious? Post-Birth Abortion! You've done nothing different than the so-called "physician" performing a third trimester abortion. Using the argument for supporting abortion the only thing you should be charged with is practicing medicine without a license.

Those who profess to be Christians cannot possibly be pro-abortion or, as many like to call themselves, "pro-choice". The truth is pro-choice is pro-abortion! From the Christian perspective abortion cannot be condoned. According to Matthew 1, ...[20] But while he thought on these things, behold, the angel of the LORD appeared unto him in a dream, saying, Joseph, thou son of David, fear not to take unto thee Mary thy wife: for that which is conceived in her is of the Holy Ghost. [21] And she shall bring forth a son, and thou shalt call his name JESUS. From the absolute Christian standpoint the soul is present at conception as indicated in this scripture. Once again, the elitists in the guise of pseudo-Christians are influencing the courts to pervert, control or destroy the values and traditions this country is built on.

The basis for almost all man-made laws, are the Ten Commandments! Some have trouble understanding this. History shows Moses came down from the mountain carrying stone tablets of which the Ten Commandments were carved. Since that time, as history indicates, almost all laws have been developed with those in mind. These Commandments do not promote a religion but rather establishes man's pecking order and standards of behavior. This is what the United States Declaration of Independence and Constitution was based on. Read the Federalists papers and other personal writings of the founding fathers and all doubt will be removed. A recent ruling from the activist members of the Supreme Court ruled according to their desires or influences not on the tradition of the past 200 years. In the case of the Ten Commandments being displayed in a Kentucky courthouse, Justices Stevens, Ginsburg, Souter and O'Connor provided, "…framed copies in two Kentucky courthouses went too far in endorsing religion, the court held. Those courthouse displays are unconstitutional the justices said, because their religious content is overemphasized." While Justice Antonin Scalia released a stinging dissent in the courthouse case, declaring, "What distinguishes the rule of law from the dictatorship of a shifting Supreme Court majority is the absolutely indispensable requirement that judicial opinions be grounded in consistently applied principle."

The Court also ruled in favor of a 6-foot-granite monument on the grounds of the Texas Capitol, one of 17 historical displays on the 22-acre lot, was determined to be a legitimate tribute to the nation's legal and religious history. "Of course, the Ten Commandments are religious! They were so viewed at their inception and so remain. The monument therefore has religious significance," Chief Justice William H. Rehnquist wrote for the majority in the case involving the display outside the state capitol of

Texas. "Simply having religious content or promoting a message consistent with a religious doctrine does not run afoul of the Establishment clause," he said. This is a decision based on over 200 years of American history and tradition. On the other hand for the activist Justices dissenting in the Texas case, Justice John Paul Stevens argued the display was an improper government endorsement of religion. Stevens noted in large letters the monument proclaims 'I AM the LORD thy God.'" This country is founded on Judeo-Christian values and hold them dearly which is clearly seen in the U.S. Constitution and Declaration of Independence.

The Declaration of Independence begins, "When in the Course of human events, it becomes necessary for one people to dissolve the political bands which have connected them with another, and to assume among the powers of the earth, the separate and equal station to which the Laws of Nature and of **Nature's God** entitle them…"! The second paragraph begins, "We hold these truths to be self-evident, that all men are created equal, that they are **endowed by their Creator** with certain unalienable Rights, that among these are Life, Liberty and the pursuit of Happiness.--That to secure these rights, Governments are instituted among Men, deriving their just powers from the consent of the governed…"!

Think of the significance of these rulings concerning the mention of God. How long will it be before the extremists, elitists and pseudo-Christians push the issue of making the Declaration of Independence unconstitutional? Think it can't happen? Think again! The groundwork has been laid for rulings against any mention of God in the government setting. It will come if we let it. Now, it's time to ask yourself, "Are you a true Christian, Jew or Muslim or are you a pseudo-Christian, pseudo-Jew, or pseudo-Muslim?" Your answer lay in the way you live your life and your actions toward others. The wrong decision may cost you eternity!

Another recent Supreme Court decision which appears to be an all out assault on individual rights is the New London, Connecticut decision* allowing local governments to take away your property and sell it to another private citizen or company to increase tax benefits and tourism dollars. Maybe the justices who ruled for this didn't learn about American History. The "Boston Tea Party" comes to mind. America gained independence primarily due to unfair taxation and the haves oppressing the have-nots. This decision returns us to the pre-Revolutionary War society.

Wait, Justices David H. Souter, Ruth Bader Ginsburg and Stephen G. Breyer, as well Justice Anthony Kennedy did uphold the Constitution. Under Article 11 "[State Property](1) State property, i.e. the common property of the…people, is the principal form of…property. (2) The land, its minerals, waters, and forests are the exclusive property of the state. The state owns the basic means of production in industry, construction, and agriculture; means of transport and communication; the banks; the property of state-run trade organizations and public utilities, and other state-run undertakings; most urban housing; and other property necessary for state purposes." Or an even better justification is Article 13 "[Personal Property] paragraph (3) Property owned or used by citizens shall not serve as a means of deriving unearned income or be employed to the detriment of the interests of society."

What? You say you don't remember seeing this in the Constitution? Well, open your eyes. This is clear as day in the Constitution of the Former Soviet Union of 1917, 1925 (revised), and finally 1977. You can easily read Article 11 and 13 under Section 2 of this document. As Justice Scalia has stated, "…the Court has essentially liberated itself from the text of the Constitution, from the text and even from the traditions of the American people." Some of these Justices are basing decisions on laws from outside the United States. For example, take a 2003 ABC interview in which Justice O'Connor made it clear that, in her mind, the Constitution is definitely not the final word in governing America. When she was asked if there might come a day when the US Constitution would no longer be the last word on the law, she answered, "Well, you always have the power of entering into treaties with other nations which also become part of the law of the land, but I can't see the day when we won't have a constitution in our nation." Justice O'Connor apparently displays her stupidity in this matter. I would say ignorance but that would mean she didn't know any better. How could she possibly disregard the U.S. Constitution Article VI. Second paragraph which states, "This Constitution, and the Laws of the United States which shall be made in Pursuance thereof; and all Treaties made, or which shall be made, under the authority of the United States, shall be the supreme Law of the Land; and the Judges in every State shall be bound thereby, **any Thing in the Constitution or Laws of any State to the Contrary notwithstanding.**" This very simply means the Constitution takes precedence over treaties with other countries. This is extremely important as the elitists are blanketing the public with the notion that any treaty entered into overrides the Constitution. This notion is absolutely wrong. The Bill of Rights is not submissive to any treaty! Read the Federalist Papers for clarity on this.

At an awards dinner in Atlanta in October 2003, "American courts need to pay more attention to international legal decisions to help create a more favorable impression abroad", said U.S. Supreme Court Justice O'Connor. "The impressions we create in this world are important, and they can leave their mark," O'Connor said, according to the Atlanta Journal-Constitution.

The 73-year-old justice and some of her high court colleagues have made similar appeals to foreign law, not only in speeches and interviews, but in some of their legal opinions. In the past, when liberals who believe the Constitution is a "living document" wrote their opinions, they produced political and sociological explanations to support them. Now they have become as bold as to quote chapter and verse from the European Court of Human Rights. The words, actions and rulings by Justices O'Connor, Breyer, Kennedy, Ruth Bader Ginsburg, David H. Souter and John Paul Stevens is a clear violation of their oath of office, "…protect and defend the Constitution…" in their attempt to sacrifice the sovereignty of the United States and subject our citizens to laws of other countries and specifically the United Nations! Their actions alone are treasonous and are impeachable offenses. You see, when a constitutionalist writes an opinion, he or she cites the Article and Clause of the Constitution that supports it. That is the mandate of the Court's decisions. This irritates the anti-Americans to no end. The 2003 ABC television interview marked the first time sitting Supreme Court Justices (Breyer and O'Connor) have taken to the airwaves to attack the position of another Justice (Scalia) for his "literal" interpretations in his rulings.

In the past such disagreements have been confined to chambers and to the relatively civil majority and dissenting published opinions of the members. Never in my memory has any Justice violated this Court tradition by publicly attacking another Justice. It appears, in effect, the Justices were lobbying the public to support their position on a Texas case of which they had just ruled*. Plain and simple, they were playing politics, which is strictly forbidden to Justices under the doctrine of Separation of Powers.

The whole flawed concept the Constitution is a "living document" is an attempt by the far left to guide the direction of our nation away from it's traditions. Anyone with any historical education knows the founding fathers built safeguards for changing the constitution. This is what's called "Amendments". This safeguard is in place to ensure trivial changes would be difficult as is what is popular for the day. Popular of the day is what the elitists are. They know the overwhelming majority of Americans will not stand for the socialist changes they are attempting to implement. In order for an amendment to occur, congress must pass it with a two-thirds vote and then send it to the states. At that point, I believe, 36 states must approve the amendment. The liberal strongholds are most of the New England States, California and maybe one or two other states. Overall, only approximately 12 states are hardcore liberal. Most of the rest of the states have traditional and moderate philosophies. The possibility of a liberal amendment getting through the process is virtually non-existent! Hence, the idea of the constitution as a "living document" has come to be.

The Declaration of Independence states, "...That to secure these rights, Governments are instituted among Men, deriving their just powers from the consent of the governed, --That whenever any Form of Government becomes destructive of these ends, it is the Right of the People to alter or to abolish it, and to institute new Government, laying its foundation on such principles and organizing its powers in such form, as to them shall seem most likely to effect their Safety and Happiness. Prudence, indeed, will dictate that Governments long established should not be changed for light and transient causes; and accordingly all experience hath shewn, that mankind are more disposed to suffer, while evils are sufferable, than to right themselves by abolishing the forms to which they are accustomed". The far left fail to understand the above exert. They are indeed attempting to undermine, circumvent and destroy our constitutional foundations and make our country submissive to the laws of other nations.

These elitist justices seem to feel they are above the law and can create law from the bench. According to The Chronicle of Higher Education, September 13, 1999, Justice Ginsburg said, "But I am uneasy about classes in which students learn entirely from home, in front of a computer screen, with no face-to-face interaction with other students and instructors." Why do you think this is? As stated in a previous chapter, people like Justice Ginsburg want students of law to be indoctrinated into the far left mentality. By an individual taking internet classes they are learning the constitution and letter of the law without the socialist pollution that is so prevalent in our schools of higher learning. As I said before, if you are capable of passing the State Bar, then you should not be prevented from practicing law. Justice Ginsburg apparently doesn't want people to learn only the law as it's meant to be but wants everyone to be brainwashed to her way of thinking.

Absurd rulings aren't confined to just the Supreme Court but many others also. The Ninth Circuit Court of Appeals is one of the most irreverent courts in the country. On June 26, 2002, in the case of Newdow v. United States Congress, the ultra-liberal Ninth Circuit Court of Appeals came out with a ruling declaring the Pledge of Allegiance unconstitutional because of the words "under God" that were added by Congress in 1954. February 2003, the Ninth Circuit Court of Appeals refused to rehear its June ruling. In fact, the Court went on to further amend the June ruling and held that a California public school district's policy of opening each school day with the voluntary recitation of the Pledge of Allegiance "impermissibly coerces a religious act" on the part of those students who choose not to recite the pledge.

On March 12, 2003, the House Judiciary Committee, reported out H.Res.132. This bill expresses the sense of the House of Representatives that the phrase "one Nation, under God" should remain in the Pledge of Allegiance. H.Res.132 also expresses the sense of the House that the Ninth Circuit Court of Appeals decisions in Newdow v. United States Congress are inconsistent with the Supreme Court's interpretation of the First Amendment. If the initial June ruling wasn't bad enough, the second February ruling contradicts any reasonable interpretation of the First Amendment. Not surprisingly, these verdicts come from the circuit court that holds the dubious distinction of being reversed by the Supreme Court more than any other circuit in recent history!

The Pledge of Allegiance is not a religious statement or prayer, but instead, it is a statement of allegiance to the ideas and principles on which our nation was founded. No one is required to recite the Pledge, and if anyone disagrees with it or chooses to refrain from saying it, he or she is free to do so. But these two Ninth Circuit Court decisions have the effect of preventing those who want to recite the Pledge from being able to do so. This is wrong.

A ruling from Judge Alvin K. Hellerstein in September 15, 2004, Declaring that "no one is above the law," ordered the government to turn over or identify within 30 days all documents relating to the treatment of prisoners held by the United States at military bases and other detention facilities overseas, including Guantánamo Bay and Abu Ghraib. The American Civil Liberties Union and the New York Civil Liberties Union greeted the strongly worded order as a signal victory in their nearly year-long effort to compel the government to comply with their request under the Freedom of Information Act (FOIA). "The court today vindicated the public's right to know who is responsible for the systemic abuse of detainees held in United States custody," said Amrit Singh, an ACLU attorney. "The truth must be known, no matter how embarrassing it might be to the government." This is a total disregard for the constitution as enemy combatants do not fall under any jurisdiction of the judiciary. The Geneva Convention is the applicable document for these detainees. Once again you see the anti-American bias of the ACLU and their lackeys in the courts.

It doesn't stop on the national issues. For example, "in 1998, a group of people headed by Tramm Hudson, the former chairman of the Sarasota Florida County Republican Party*, got together to support the 'Two Will Do' term limits effort there. Like at least eight other counties in Florida, 68% of the people in Sarasota County thought that escaping the pitfalls of having career politicians was a good thing and approved an amendment limiting the terms of their county commissioners to two. The will of the people had been done."

"In January of 2005 a Circuit Judge ruled that the Florida Constitution does not allow for citizens to place a limit on how many times a county commissioner can be elected to office. His ruling was issued despite the fact that term limits are already in place in more than eight other Florida counties. He based his ruling on a 2002 Supreme Court decision that stated that only the state constitution could establish rules such as term limits for constitutional officers. The Judge used a broad and liberal interpretation to include county commissioners into the realm of constitutional officers."

Arguably, this could be construed as a judge creating law which is judicial activism rather than ruling on a point of law which is the judiciary's intended function. One commissioner, when asked about the Judge's decision said that she wasn't convinced that voters really meant what they voted for. "People vote for things in the heat of the moment," she said. She went on to say that she believed the voters meant for term limits to affect those in national office and that the will of the people, as mandated by their overwhelming approval of the term limits amendment, didn't apply to her or her fellow commissioners. How convenient, and very elitist of this commissioner for saying this!

This chapter has provided you with a very small sampling of the unconstitutional rulings we are seeing in our courts. The federal courts are bad enough but it even gets worse in the lower courts. Congress has the power to control the courts as stated in the Constitution Article III. "Section 1. The judicial Power of the United States, shall be vested in one supreme Court, and in such inferior Courts as the Congress may from time to time ordain and establish. The Judges, both of the supreme and inferior Courts, shall hold their Offices during good Behavior..." Violation of the oath of office is not considered good behavior. We the people have the power to tell congress to correct the deficiencies in the courts. All we have to do is remind Congress they work for us and not the special interest groups such as the ACLU and other far left anti-American elitists.

Plato (427 BC - 347 BC) said it best, "One of the penalties for refusing to participate in politics is that you end up being governed by your inferiors.

CHAPTER TEN

Nature
God's Checks and Balances

Nature entails many different aspects of our lives from where and how we live in the world to diseases and to natural disasters. Let's start at the bottom and work up to the bigger picture. One part of the extreme left is the environmentalists or "greenies"! Care of the environment is the responsibility of everyone. Unfortunately, many of the environmental activists do not understand our charge in protecting and maintaining the environment. God gave man dominion over all animals and land and granted us responsible stewardship as conservationists of these resources. Granted, many do not take this responsibility as serious as we should. Governments are the last ones we should expect any responsible actions from. Environmentalists are right up there with government in harming the environment.

First, you must understand what the difference is between an environmentalist and a conservationist. An environmentalist is one who has studied the environment in school and through books and even may have a little experience in the field. A conservationist is essentially one who is raised and/or lives in the environment as part of it and also may have studied about the environment through school, etc…! The difference is quiet clear and after seeing this definition many environmentalists will claim to be conservationists. One cannot be a conservationist if their arguments for the environment exclude humans from being part of the environment.

Think about Nature for a minute. Any notion man has that he is in control of the world and environment is absurdity and arrogance at best. Nature is very forgiving until pushed too far. God designed Nature to be resilient and to react to threats in a fitting fashion. The greenies don't understand this as they "feel" man has to take control of the environment and to do this the enlightened must dictate to the rest of us how to live. A perfect example for this is the "sustainable development" concept to promote "high density housing" and "green zones" or "green infrastructure". This concept is the brainchild of the United Nations* Conference on Human Settlements (Habitat I), held in Vancouver. Essentially, the idea is to herd the population into concentrated housing areas and create these green zones which are devoid of human presence.

At a meeting at the Birmingham, Alabama Hilton on April 8, 2003, very few people knew that the objective of the meeting was to implement U.N. policy in Alabama*. Most of those in attendance was under the impression the meeting was to solicit comments about a "forest management plan" under development by the U.S. Fish and Wildlife Service. A comment period was open until July, at which time the plan was to go into effect to standardize "ecosystem management" in all national forests in Alabama. "When asked if the plan provided for core wilderness areas, surrounded by buffer zones," spokesman for the government, answered "Yes"! "The plan fulfills the criteria of Article 4 of UNESCO's 'Statutory Framework for U.N. Biosphere Reserves.' "Most of Alabama has already been gobbled up by the Southern Appalachian Biosphere Reserve, one of 47 U.N. Biosphere Reserves designated in the U.S., with no debate, discussion or vote by any state legislature or the U.S. Congress."

A major function of all U.N. Biosphere Reserves is to continually expand the core wilderness areas by confiscating private property, one way or another, and connecting corridors of wilderness, with the intent of pushing the buffer zones further and further outward. Once this happens the plan is to create a "zone of cooperation" which will continually expand. "The Southern Appalachian Reserve began with the designation of the 517,000-acre Great Smoky Mountains National Park as a U.N. Biosphere

Reserve. State Department maps now show the reserve to include an area that stretches from Birmingham to Roanoke, and from Nashville to Asheville".

I can hear many of you saying, "Oh, no, another nut blaming the UN. Do your own research and you will see what is being done right under your nose. This is another attempt to control you, your property and the way you live. These people use "junk science" to try and justify these grandiose plans. I've heard the local "planners" say by implementing high density housing it will preserve the environment as it will provide for more "open spaces" and provide our children a more natural environment. This is completely wrong. They fail to mention the results of dense population. Diseases are spread more easily when people's proximity to one another is roof top to roof top. Why do you think the "Black Plague" ravaged Europe, the Middle East, China and parts of Northern Africa in the fourteenth century. It was spread primarily through trade routes and then concentrated in the densely populated areas. Europe lost about a third of its population and one province in China lost about 90 percent of its population. Why? Ignorance of how the disease spread and dense housing accommodations! The countryside (farmers and families) remained virtually untouched. Look at the incidence of colds, the flu and other contagious disease in heavily populated areas compared to the rural environment. Big difference!

Nature has a way of correcting wrongs, especially wrongs created by man. Almost a generation ago man "conquered" small pox. We thought that was a great feat, which it was at the time. A short time later another disease hit us like a ton of bricks. AIDS came on the scene with a vengeance. This is a great example of Nature's checks and balances. We think we take control and then Nature will come back to let us know we aren't in control. The far left fail to understand this!

Getting back to how the greenies are trying to dictate where and how we live. Many of these people want to "save the forests". That's their reasoning to force people into the dense housing they propose in many zoning plans throughout the country. If you look at the science of these "plans" it is plain to see how flawed they are and the real reason becomes all the more apparent. Using a model developed by The Shodor Education Foundation, Inc*. in cooperation with the North Carolina State University Cooperative Extension Service Neuse River Education Team one can calculate water runoff. This model allows you to calculate water runoff for many different environments ranging from residential, paved streets, gravel roads, woods and forests to farmland. Using this model and all factors of rainfall, duration, quantity and soil type being the same, it was determined that water runoff for a house on a half acre lot (residential) was four times that of farmstead on approximately 2 acres. What is the impact of this? A farm generally doesn't use many chemicals and what is used is readily absorbed by the environment. The residential, on the other hand, typically uses more herbicides, chemical fertilizers, concrete cleaners, frequent car washes and so on. These chemicals are washed into the water table during a rain which is devastating to the eco-system. Many of the people living in these developments are the very ones who are screaming about saving the environment. It would be more environmentally sound to restrict houses be built on lots no smaller than 2 acres with minimal concrete and asphalt. Science has proven this to be healthier for the environment than the way developments are currently built.

I have a small farm downstream from several of these developments. When we started this farm about 8 years ago many of these developments did not exist. The creek flowing through our property was clean with an abundance of fish and shallow enough to wade to the other side without getting your shirt wet. When it rained it did rise, sometimes to the top of the banks and only flooded when we had excessive periods of rain. Over the past three years this has changed. Due to several high density housing developments which the green "planners" had a hand in pushing, the creek no longer sports as many fish. You can no longer wade through the creek as before. Many of our neighbors who've lived here for generations say the banks of the creek have eroded more in the past three years than they've seen in the past 40 years. Much of the animal life that was here only a few years ago is now gone.

We are also fortunate to live away from any main roads and access to our farm is restricted. We have taken measures to ensure our farm is environmentally sound. We refrain from using insecticides or chemicals as much as possible. One day I intercepted a county truck which was "fogging" for mosquitoes before he could get close to my farm. I told him to turn it off and leave and do not come back. He explained the people in these developments a few miles away said they wanted the county to control the mosquitoes. The method which was condoned is essentially using an insecticide or petroleum based product and killing all insects. I informed him we had several large areas of standing water but had no mosquito problem because we had an abundance of dragonflies, frogs, martins and bats which did a fantastic job at keeping the mosquito population to a manageable level. He said his college degree was in environmental areas and he had not heard of anything like this before. He was not aware of the natural predators to mosquitoes could be used to control them so well. I showed him a manure pile from our horses and asked if he saw anything unusual. He looked and after a while said he didn't see hardly any flies. I told him we used hornets (a predator to flies) to control the flies effectively. This is how we are supposed to live. We are part of Nature, not bystanders or spectators. Many of these far left environmentalists really can't understand this because most just don't live it. Besides, this would interfere with the elitists being able to exert control over you and your property.

Global warming caused by pollution created by man will destroy the world. Does anyone with any sense believe Nature will allow man to go to far? History shows Nature will retaliate and correct the wrongs mankind create. Nature targeted dinosaurs for extinction when their numbers became excessive. Many of these elitists claim the existence of dinosaurs prove there is no God as the Bible doesn't speak of dinosaurs. Once again these misinformed people have it wrong. Genesis 6:4, "There were **giants** in the earth in those days; and also after that, when the sons of God came in unto the daughters of men, and they bare children to them, the same became mighty men which were of old, men of renown." How could the author of Genesis even know about these giants (dinosaurs) at that time? There was no organized science community to promote this idea. Some will say well they got the idea from cave drawings. There are 12 other references to giants or land of the giants in the Bible. This is as significant as other scientific evidence about dinosaurs. It may very well indicate the existence of life on earth is not as old as some believe. What impact does this have on our modern times? For one it indicates all species of dinosaurs may not have become extinct during the "ice age" and casts serious doubt on modern day "fossil fuels" is a result of the decomposition of these dinosaurs. The greenies don't like this idea because then it may indicate oil is a renewable resource.

In his search for data, Dr. Thomas Gold*, performed drilling experiments that showed the presence of petroleum at depths greater than fossils might be found. Supporting evidence is present in various forms, one of which is the presence of bacteria that consume petroleum deep inside the Earth. And further support for the Gold Hypothesis is being seen today as previously dry oil fields are being refilled from beneath, a result that is consistent with his model. The significance of this is oil is the result of a naturally occurring process of which Nature has resources of dealing with, when this oil breeches areas it shouldn't. This is where man comes in as we are the ones who many times cause these breeches.

Take the oil tanker Exxon "Valdez"* which grounded on Bligh Reef, On March 24, 1989 and spilled nearly 11 million gallons of oil into the biologically rich waters of Prince William Sound. NOAA scientists and spill response experts helped to respond to this spill, and NOAA biologists have been monitoring the long-term effects of the spill and cleanup efforts. After ten years of study it was determined significant damage occurred immediately following the spill and the human response actually may have had more of a negative impact on the environment by our response to the disaster. Although, we can't say the local environment is back the way it was before it appears almost all damage has been reduced to have no further negative impact on the environment. The bulk of the cleanup was not done by man but by Nature. To give you a better understanding of how Nature corrects on "her" time clock and not ours think of it this way. Let's say it took Nature 10 years to correct this oil spill. Compare this time frame to a human being's average life and it would be equivalent to less than one second.

Look at many of the elitists attitudes toward the environment. John Kerry spoke to a crowd of environmentalists and denied driving a SUV. When confronted he said "his family" had a SUV. This type of double talk is the norm for these high profile "so-called" environmentalists. We see this over and over where the "Do as I say and not as I do" attitude permeates the elitists composition. Don't get me wrong, some of these environmentalists put their money where their mouth is. The problem is the majority, do not and their agenda is becoming clear as they want to control our lives and the way we live. The double standard which exists for these elitists is astounding. Where is the criticism of eco-terrorist attacks in our country? According to the Department of Justice, the number one terrorist threat in this country is from eco-terrorists. These people consistently bite off their nose to spite their face.

Many of these elitists are attempting to push their way of thinking on everyone else. They mistakenly feel animals are elevated to the same level a humans. You just about can't get any more anti-Christian than that. The political elitists essentially turn a blind eye to these activist terrorist activities as it provides them more reasons to restrict everyone else's rights and freedoms. Take a look at some of the paradox by these groups. Animal Liberation Front (ALF), Earth Liberation Front (ELF) and Stop Huntingdon Animal Cruelty (SHAC) seem to be some of the most radical.

ELF first claimed sole responsibility for an attack in the U.S. in 1997*, when activists burned down a Bureau of Land Management horse corral in Oregon (previous attacks had been claimed in conjunction with ALF). The following year in national headlines the group claimed responsibility for the arson of a ski resort in Vail, Colorado, causing $12 million in damages. This was the costliest act of eco-terrorism in American history up to this time. In its communiqué, ELF said, "putting profits ahead of Colorado's wildlife will not be tolerated….We will be back if this greedy corporation continues to trespass into wild and unroaded [sic] areas." Since the Vail arson, hundreds of crimes have been committed in the name of environmental protection nationwide. One of the most damaging occurred on August 1, 2003*, when arsonists burned down a housing complex under construction in San Diego, destroying a five-story building and 100-foot-high crane; losses were estimated at $50 million. A 12-foot banner reading "If you build it, we will burn it," along with the ELF acronym, was found at the scene. These arsons typified, in an especially destructive way, ELF's ongoing battle against "urban sprawl," which it views as a wasteful and unnecessary encroachment on natural habitats.

While I don't disagree with curtailing "urban sprawl" I do disagree with destructive measures used which in turn causes more harm to the environment. Car dealerships and sport utility vehicles are also common targets for ELF. On August 22, 2003, approximately 40 Hummers and SUVs were destroyed or damaged in a fire at a West Covina, California, dealership, causing about $2 million in damages. "Fat Lazy Americans" and "ELF" were among slogans painted on the vehicles. The movement has taken credit for vandalizing SUVs in dozens of other cities. At an auto dealership in Erie, Pennsylvania, for instance, jugs of gasoline were ignited under three vehicles, engulfing them and a nearby car in flames. ELF said the dealership was targeted "to remove the profit motive from the killing of the natural environment." How stupid is this statement. In a 24 hour period, these fires put more harmful pollution in the environment than all the Hummers that were destroyed could put in the environment in a year. Where is the outcry from our political elitists concerning this? They appear to use these fanatical elitists to further their agenda of controlling the average citizen. Notice how closely the agenda matches between the radical environmentalists and the policies being pushed by the United Nations.

The flawed Kyoto treaty provides more insight over how certain entities want to control Americans and redistribute our wealth to other countries around the world. If you put the Kyoto treaty* into the IPCC computer model, you find that the difference Kyoto would make by 2100 (the normal benchmark year) **cannot be measured.** That is, the predicted change in global average temperature (or pick your parameter) is so small that one could not tell, by looking at the temperature data, whether or not Kyoto had been in effect for 100 years. Looked at another way, Kyoto does not end anthropogenic warming, but only slows it down by 6 years out of 100. When reading the treaty you may also notice that Kyoto was written in a way to hurt the United States to the benefit of Western Europe, China and India and other third world countries. This is the United Nations idea of "leveling the big business playing field". In other words America sacrifices so others may prosper.

These elitists are concerned with "global warming" yet completely ignore Nature's role in pollution and its ultimate control of our environment. Take pollution from power plants. We've done a decent job of decreasing emissions from these necessary evils. Are they really that bad? Would you want to live downwind of 3,650 power plants? People on the big island in Hawaii live in a similar environment. Instead of power plants though, it's Kilauea's volcano*. The volcano spews out more than 1,000 tons of sulfur dioxide (1,200 tons, according to a recent study) and other pollutants every day, compared with about 100 tons a year from major air pollution sources elsewhere. According to "Where Volcanoes Occur" in World Book Online Reference Center there are hundreds of these volcanoes around the world. Essentially, this means Nature releases tens of thousands of times of harmful sulfur dioxide into the environment more than all the pollution man creates. Where's the outrage against Nature?

As I said before, many of these elitists only want to impose their will upon the rest of us. They like to use "junk science" to justify many of their flawed beliefs. You know the ones. They handed out leaflets at the showing of the movie "The Day After Tomorrow". Interesting work of fiction! Unfortunately many of these "greenies" take it as gospel. While we are seeing rain in the Midwest and other parts of the world increasing in saline content this theory of the ice caps in the arctic melting and desalinating the oceans has little scientific validity. As a matter of fact the salinity* of the oceans have remained fairly constant for millions of years. The salinity varies between about 32 and 37 parts per thousand (PPT). Scientists have also discovered the ice caps in the Arctic and Antarctic actually contain concentrated unfrozen pockets of salt water that reconstitutes with the ice when thawed. This alone debunks the whole "junk science" theories these environmentalists like to use. One of the theories for this movie was an ice chunk detaching from the polar cap. This actually occurred in 1995 with the Larsen B ice shelf in Antarctica breaking off with the approximate size of Rhode Island. These environmentalists were shouting the doom and gloom "global warming" rhetoric to anyone who would listen. Over the course of a few years the ice chunk broke apart, rejoined itself and continued on its journey. A few months ago this floating chunk of ice reattached to the main body in Antarctica. Did you hear anything about this? Of course not! These elitists don't like these pesky facts getting in the way of their feelings.

The fact is according to two studies* of temperatures and ice-cap movements in Antarctica suggest that the Southern Hemisphere's "canary" isn't going down without a fight - key sections of the ice cap appear to be growing thicker, not thinner, as previously believed. And the continent's average temperature appears to have cooled slightly during the past 35 years, not warmed. This flies in the face of the ravings of the environmental elitists. While we do have to be concerned with the control of pollution, the earth is not in danger of ending anytime soon. The human race, on the other hand, is doing a good job at destroying itself! We must understand we are at the mercy of Nature.

Over the past forty years, man has attempted to control elements of the weather. When we encroach into Nature's domain, we gamble with her wrath. The recent events of the Tsunami in Asia, mudslides in China, mountainsides collapsing and destroying homes in California and earthquakes occurring all over the world. We cannot stop Nature! We are only a very small insignificant part of it. The elitists are notorious for using scare tactics in their thinly veiled attempt to control your property, your habits and your life.

CHAPTER ELEVEN

Media Complicity
Or
The Squeaky Wheel Gets the Oil

Have you ever pushed a wheelbarrow or towed a trailer and heard the wheel squeak? You determine which wheel it is and then apply some lubrication to it to shut it up. If it were a perfect world and you're really attentive, you'll end up oiling all the wheels to ensure all receive the same coverage and protection. This is reflective of the major media in America. Not only do the major networks foster an anti-American mentality but they are quick to cover the special interest groups (squeaky wheels) especially when it boosts their agenda.

Since we do not live in a perfect world the media seems to focus much of their attention on these squeaky wheels and almost entirely ignores the rest. This elitist mentality is known as "group think". These people live in areas like New York, Washington DC, Boston, Philadelphia, Los Angeles, San Francisco, Atlanta, Miami, and many other densely populated areas. These people are surrounded by others who think the same way they do. They are blinded by this "group think" they can't even see how biased they have become in their reporting of the news. Facts deteriorate into opinion and when they do get a fact, it gets hammered to death. A good example of this is the New York Times has run about 60 front page headlines about Abu Ghraib abuses of prisoners by US military. Every time Senator Kennedy blasts the abuses at Abu Ghraib the liberal media runs another front page story. This bolsters their anti-American crusade.

Newsweek ran with a story about a Koran being flushed down a toilet by a US Military guard at Guantanamo without verifying the accuracy of the story. When it came to light this did not happen, Newsweek was slow to recant. Dan Rather at CBS ran a story with questionable documents indicating President Bush failed to complete his Air National Guard commitment in the 1960s. These documents were supposedly received from a questionable source and later determined to be forgeries. Yet, Dan Rather stood by the story for a week. He is so anti-President Bush he wanted it to be true. When the truth could no longer be denied by CBS, Mr. Rather indicated the intent was true even if the documents were not. How much more blatantly biased can these elitists be? And the pathetic thing is these people do not think they are doing anything wrong in telling what is known to be lies.

Why do the media act in this manner? Most likely because they want all the bad things about America and the Bush Administration to be true they will ignore good sense and print fabrications or when they actually have something factual, beat it into the ground. Look at how the media treats other stories or groups. Has the media provided coverage or even exhibit an interest in, say, the Veterans of Foreign Wars? This organization has over 2.4 million members and offices throughout the United States. This number is representative of a good portion of veterans of foreign wars. Many of the local chapters provide assistance to the needy and disabled war veterans. How often is one of their stories covered? What about their efforts to work with congress to provide better benefits to those Americans who've served their country. Who in the media are reporting about the homeless veterans and how we can help them rejoin society? I find it distressing the media refuses to cover an organization that is attempting to care for those who've given so much. One factor is this organization doesn't beat its chest screaming from the rooftops of how mistreated some of their members are. They are not a squeaky wheel in comparison to the smaller liberal groups who receive a warm reception from the elite media. VFW members have sacrificed for this country and are used to getting the short end of the stick. Why should scant media attention be any different?

How about the coverage of the Boy Scouts? The only thing I've seen in the media the last few years is how the Boy Scouts have been under attack by the ACLU. Do you hear anything positive about the Boy Scouts? Membership is about a million young men strong with about half a million adult volunteers. One program is the Good Turn concept which is a major part of the personal growth method of Boy Scouting. Boys grow as they participate in community service projects and do Good Turns for others. This is probably the most successful device in developing a basis for personal growth. The religious emblems program also is a large part of the personal growth method. Frequent personal conferences with his Scoutmaster help each Boy Scout to determine his growth toward Scouting's aims. Do you hear about these good deeds? Of course not! You do hear about exclusion of homosexuals and how the ACLU has been successful at having the Boy Scouts thrown out of a public park in California. For some reason, the media just doesn't report the good deeds performed daily by the Boy Scouts. These are just two organizations which historically have been the shining light for what is good in America. There are many more but you can research this on your own.

Let's talk about the squeaky wheels. The ACLU is a good one to start with. With membership around 330,000 the ACLU seem to be well funded by special interest groups seeking to change the direction of America. How can the low membership pay for the legal maneuvers of the ACLU? Either all the members are filthy rich or there are a lot of special interests with big bucks behind them. They do receive some government grants, which I believe should be reviewed and eliminated as this organization acts predominantly against Americans interests. The ACLU* was founded at a party attended by Socialist Party notable Norman Thomas, future Communist Party chairman Elizabeth Gurley Flynn, and Soviet agent Agnes Smedley. The ACLU claims to be an unbiased, "Neither conservative nor liberal" organization devoted exclusively to protecting the civil liberties of all Americans. But their record proves just the opposite. Under the guise of 'protecting American civil rights', Baldwin's ACLU has sued to; Halt the singing of Christmas Carols in public facilities. Deny tax exempt status for Churches. Remove all military chaplains. Remove all Christian symbols from public property. Prohibit Bible reading in classrooms even during free time. Remove "In God We Trust" from our coins. Remove God from the Pledge of Allegiance. Deny federal funding for Boy Scouts until they admit gays and atheists. The ACLU's holy war against the Boy Scouts, the LA County Official Seal which contains a tiny Cross, holidays like Thanksgiving and Christmas, and even the Constitution itself, has unmasked the ACLU as a tyrant less interested in civil rights than imposing judicial restraints that amount to suppression of majority rights by a tiny minority.

"The ACLU must extinguish America's fundamental belief in God, in order for the ACLU to tear down constitutional barriers to governmental power since such a belief is an essential denial of the supreme power of government. According to the Declaration of Independence, rights come from God, not government. When God's presence in the American mindset ceases, however, people no longer look to God as the grantor of rights but to government. Therefore, the ACLU argues that the more power the government has, the better off the people under it are. The ACLU has been so successful, that if the argument is framed properly, the Declaration of Independence can be interpreted as unconstitutional. Thanks to the ACLU a San Francisco suburban teacher* was forbidden to give out copies of the Declaration of Independence to his students by the school's principal, because it refers to God. The Principal has also required that the teacher clear all his lessons first with her."

Why does the ACLU get all the media attention? For one it promotes the elite media's anti-America bias and another is pushing the socialist agenda on America. It's one of the loudest squeaky wheels.

The ACLU does a marvelous job at integrating the Constitution of the former Soviet Union into the fabric of America to further their agenda.

Another one is the National Organization for Women (NOW) with a membership of around 500,000. Once again, another fairly small organization with a loud voice the media seems to promote. There are approximately 144,500,000 women in the United States. NOW claims to represent them. How in the world can .0034602 percent represent the other 99.99654 percent of the women? The champion of women's rights! According to the NOW website, "NOW's goal has been to take action to bring about equality for all women. NOW works to eliminate discrimination and harassment in the workplace, schools, the justice system, and all other sectors of society; secure abortion, birth control and reproductive rights for all women; end all forms of violence against women; eradicate racism, sexism and homophobia; and promote equality and justice in our society." Perhaps it can be explained better as rights like, the right to murder unborn children, destruction of the family by encouraging women not to be family oriented. Secure abortion, birth control and reproductive rights for all women but who is speaking for the unborn?

Women did need help to be heard about 40 years ago, NOW managed to hurt women rather than help. Equality was their goal or so they said. Historically, men placed women on a pedestal. In many respects feminism has removed that pedestal. This was ignored by the media for the most part because if men held women in such high regard the destruction of the family could not be accomplished. The media would have you believe most men treated women as lesser. Nothing could be farther from the truth except in the dens of densely populated areas where immorality was rampant.

The elitists, who populated many of these areas, erroneously believed everyone else thought the same way. The truth is, in "flyover country", the majority of people are God fearing and respectful of each others role in life. Well, these elitists can't have this! No, they not only had to drag women off the pedestal but misinformed them about love, life, country and God. Women are truly equal thanks to these misguided elitists. The number one killer of women was breast cancer until a very short time ago. Now women enjoy being killed by the number one killer of men, heart disease! Thanks to organization such as NOW women have equality in the market place and our future generations are deteriorating. Instead of emphasis being placed on the most important aspect of our future (raising children), emphasis was placed on self accomplishment. It's no wonder we have seen an increase in juvenile crime, drug use, immoral behavior, many more ills of our young in society and destruction of families. The feminists just don't get it. A woman who forgoes success in the business world to raise a family accomplishes much more and has a more profound impact on the future of the world through her children. That is greater than any success in the business world. How can these groups be so well financed? Either all their members are wealthy or the deep pockets of these elitists are paying the bills. Again, why does an organization with such low membership get so much attention? Maybe because of how loud they scream and how sympathetic the media is to their cause!

Homosexual rights happen to be another squeaky wheel that gets a lot of attention. The media has promoted the homosexual agenda. Anyone who disagrees is labeled a homophobe. These elitists want you to believe homosexuals comprise over 10 percent of our population. To give you an idea to show this is not true, I want to give you an exercise to try. Pretend 9 out of every 10 black people you see is a homosexual. I said pretend! I suggest the black population because this percentage is close to the figure the media is pushing for the percentage of homosexuals in our country. As you can see this is absolutely not possible. After significant research*, the number of homosexuals is closer to about 1.5 to 3 percent of the population

with the heaviest concentrations in New
York, San Francisco and several other
large cities. This reflects a more
accurate figure of between 4.3 million to
8.7 million. New York leads the way with
approximately 600,000 homosexuals, which
appears much closer to the correct number
than the media attempts to report. The
many falsehoods associated with the
homosexual population seem to be
propagated by the media.

One of the main topics the media has
not been forthright about is HIV/AIDS.
This disease was unusual to begin with as
it appeared to "target" a deviant
lifestyle. You wouldn't know this by the
media reports in the past 20 years. Here
is what the media has failed to report
about this disease. History of AIDS
indicates the virus was present in monkey
years earlier and the virus was first
spread to humans through hunting and
eating of the contaminated meat.
Scientists claim that AIDS may have
lingered in the African population for
decades only exploding when the continent
was colonized and urbanized. As people
moved from the forest to towns and
cities, they brought the virus with them.
And evolving, new methods of rapid
transportation helped spread it around
the world. Supposedly an airline steward
who reportedly participated in wild "sex
parties" had a role in spreading it to
others who lived this type of lifestyle.
Homosexuals in New York were the first to

develop AIDS in 1981 and it spread like wildfire through the homosexual community. Some were drug users, some donated blood, some just wanted others to suffer, all of which caused the spread of the disease. This is an easily preventable disease. For some reason many on the far left use scare tactics in order to bring attention to this disease and for funding of research for a cure. While it is a serious disease and many innocents have been infected the extremists have misrepresented* this to the rest of us in the spread of the disease through the heterosexual community.

The heterosexual community, for the most part, acted responsibly in preventing the spread of this disease while the homosexual community only backed off for a while. Unfortunately, there are those who just don't get it. According to news reports the Center for Disease Control reported a more intense strain of HIV occurring in a number of homosexual men in New York City within the past year. Instead of years to convert to AIDS this one takes months and the lethality seems to be quicker. Have you heard this reported in the mainstream media lately? Of course not! The elite media will most likely suppress the reporting of this new strain until it infects some heterosexuals or drug users who share needles. At this point it will fit their agenda for pushing for more funding.

More money is spent on research for a cure to this horrific disease than spent on research for breast cancer for women, yet, more women die from breast cancer every year than people from AIDS. Some people don't see anything wrong with this. AIDS is an easily preventable disease but people don't want to change their lifestyle and all of us have to suffer. Breast cancer is not easily preventable and women who contract it have no choice. I'm not bashing homosexuals, I'm bashing irresponsible behavior that is resulting in the death and suffering of people, many who don't deserve this fate. The elite media apparently refuses to act responsibly in reporting these facts until they can use it for their agenda.

The media also seems to promote the left leaning AARP. The media has given AARP plenty of air time concerning President Bush's Social Security private accounts. The AARP seems to be dead set against this plan. What the media is not reporting is the AARP is promoting their own private accounts for seniors. In simple words, seniors who use the AARP resources benefit, as well as the AARP. If the government promotes and oversees these private accounts, the AARP essentially will lose money. They apparently need these funds to continue lobbying for liberal issues not directly related to seniors. Do you want more taxes taken out of your earnings? Do you want more unelected bureaucrats taking over more details of your life and your family's life? Do you want federal regulators making your health choices, instead of you, your family, and your doctor? Do you want government regulators to control the investment and retirement decisions of your family, instead of you? If you answered "Yes," then AARP is your group. As Art Linkletter states, "They continuously work to create high taxes, big, invasive, bloated government, herds of regulators, and dependency of citizens on unelected bureaucrats." The AARP's philosophies fall right in line with the elite media. Perhaps they want the higher taxes in the hopes of receiving more taxpayer money. AARP reportedly has received over one billion taxpayer dollars over the past 20 years.

Have you heard of USA Next? The media overlooks this organization for seniors. Perhaps, it could be due to the USA Next philosophy reflects what many traditional Americans want. Do you want lower taxes, more control over your life, health, and finances, with less government, and more constitutional restraints on judges and unelected bureaucrats? Then discontinue your AARP membership and join USA Next so they can work and fight for you! This definitely doesn't correspond with the elite media.

Have you seen the media report anything positive about the Thomas More Law Center? The Thomas More Law Center is a not-for-profit public interest law firm dedicated to the defense and promotion of the religious freedom of Christians, time-honored family values, and the sanctity of human life. They provide legal representation without charge to defend and protect Christians and their religious beliefs in the public square. Where's the media reporting on the successes of this group? You won't hear about it because it contradicts the elitists philosophy of God must be removed from the public arena so they can control you and me.

The disparity in media coverage between conservatives and liberals is also an area of concern. Look at the media frenzy over Trent Lott when he attended the 100th birthday celebration of Strom Thurmond. Mr. Lott said, "I want to say this about my state: When Strom Thurmond ran for president, we voted for him. We're proud of it. And if the rest of the country had followed our lead, we wouldn't have had all these problems over all these years, either." Granted, a poor choice of words was used but the media went into a feeding frenzy over this. Even, when he issued the apology, "A poor choice of words conveyed to some the impression that I embraced the discarded policies of the past, nothing could be further from the truth, and I apologize to anyone who was offended by my statement." This still did not stop the onslaught. The media frenzy continued until Mr. Lott stepped down from his position as House Majority Leader.

Look at how the media covered Robert Byrd (D), West Virginia. In a 2001 interview with Tony Snow of Fox News, Mr. Byrd said, "…There are white niggers. I've seen a lot of white niggers in my time; I'm going to use that word." Where was the media outrage over this? Another liberal gaff by Howard Dean during a meeting with the Democratic black caucus, Dean praised black Democrats for their work for the party, then questioned Republicans' ability to rally support from minorities. "You think the Republican National Committee could get this many people of color in a single room?" Dean asked to laughter, "Only if they had the hotel staff in here." Did the attendees realize Mr. Dean just insulted them? Where was the media outrage over either of these overtly racist statements by Mr. Byrd and Mr. Dean? These are just a few incidents about the liberal bias in the media and the complicity of the elitists to further their agenda.

For over 40 years the media has been assisting other elitists in stacking the deck against traditional America through the courts and in the media. Perversion of the Constitution and infiltrating higher schools of learning, especially law schools with socialist minded teachers has been some of the main instruments these elitists have used. The complicity of the elite media to destroy traditions grounded in American culture and establish new Godless traditions is becoming more and more evident. These pseudo-Christians fail to understand, to God, your everyday actions reflect your reverence or irreverence to God. No one is perfect and we do have a forgiving God, but if you live and/or promote immorality, I believe there is a limit to God's forgiveness. If you are one of those who wish to rid our government of God, you will have an eternity to contemplate how wrong you are.

CHAPTER TWELVE

The Face of Evil

There is more than one face of evil. Some will say Bill Clinton or George Bush is the face of evil. If you are one of those who believe this, you are wrong. Both Bill Clinton and George Bush have done and continue to do what they believe is best for the country. Their actions and accomplishments bear this to be true. Although you may not agree or like one or the other, they have not oppressed, persecuted or enslaved any people. There are others on the world stage that have oppressed and to some degree enslaved and persecuted people either through inaction or passive complicity.

It really boils down to anyone or any organization that wants to impede freedoms, restrict individual rights, redistribute wealth, and disregard the sovereignty of any nation is a face of evil. The United States has led the world in delivering freedom to millions of people. You wouldn't know this by listening to the elitists. Take Ted Kennedy (I'm sure he represents someone's face of evil) who routinely bashes the accomplishments of the U.S. Military. He has not defended our country and by all accounts it appears he has raped this country with the help of his elitist friends. The "tunnel" project is billions of dollars over budget. Even though the "tunnel" isn't open its already sprouting leaks, meaning, more money will be dumped into this boondoggle. That is money we could have spent on disease research, job programs, assistance for the economically depressed. To hear him talk you would think he is the champion to these causes. What can you expect from the son of a man who, in 1938, advised the President that Adolph Hitler was not a threat? All politicians garner a little pork for their constituents, usually to the tune of a few million dollars NOT billions of dollars. One may ask, "Is this truly the face of evil?" Look at his actions now and go all the way back to Chappaquiddick where it was reported he was drunk and drove off a bridge resulting in the death of a young lady. I believe I can honestly say if I were in that situation, I would have been sent to jail. Look into his history and you make the call.

One could say for another serious face of evil look at the founder of Planned Parenthood, Margaret Sanger. While the elite media and supporters of abortion rights have done their best to hide it, the fact is Sanger perverted Darwinian logic to its extreme, just as the Nazis did in Germany. During the 1930s Sanger openly supported the Nazi's goal of achieving eugenics to create what was supposed to be a "super race." In truth, Planned Parenthood's 1985 "Annual Report"

proclaimed members were, "Proud of our past, and planning for our future." Several notable goals and sayings of Margaret Sanger are listed:
- She wrote that society needed to go about the task of the "extermination of 'human weeds' ...the 'cessation of charity,' ... the segregation of 'morons, misfits, and the maladjusted,' and ... the sterilization of 'genetically inferior races.'" ("Killer Angel"* page 65)
- Sanger publicly lauded Hitler's theory of Aryan white supremacy. (Pivot of Civilization*)
- Sanger commissioned Ernst Rudin, a member of the Nazi Party who would later become the director of the German Medical Experimentation Programs; he served Sanger's advisor until the hostilities leading to W.W.II broke out. (Pivot of Civilization*)
- Sanger opened one of her early birth control clinics in the Brownsville section of New York; the reason apparently was because this area was populated by newly immigrated Slavs, Latins, Italians, and Jews — groups she considered inferior to other races. (Woman's Body, Woman's Right*, p204.)
- In 1939, Margaret Sanger organized a "Negro project" to eliminate what she called an "inferior race." She claimed, "The masses of Negroes ...particularly in the South, still breed carelessly and disastrously, with the result that the increase among Negroes, even more than

among whites, is from that portion of the population least intelligent and fit." (Woman's Body, Woman's Right*, p. 332.)

- Sanger wrote that she intended to hire three or four Afro-American ministers "to travel to various black enclaves to propagandize for birth control…. The most successful educational approach to the Negro is through a religious appeal. We do not want word to go out that we want to exterminate the Negro population, and the Minister is the man who can straighten out that idea if it ever occurs to any of their more rebellious members." (Killer Angel*, p. 74.)

- Sanger also wrote that religious groups should be singled out for destruction because they were "dysgenic races" which included "Fundamentalists and Catholics" as well as "blacks, Hispanics, (and) American Indians." (Woman's Body, Woman's Right*, pp. 229-334)

- Sanger wrote, "Birth control appeals to the advanced radical because it is calculated to undermine the authority of the Christian churches. I look forward to seeing humanity free someday of the tyranny of Christianity no less than Capitalism." (Killer Angel*, p. 104.)

Its no wonder the elitists hide their heroine's true beliefs. Perhaps we are seeing the true agenda behind one portion of the elitists agenda of destroying "inferior races" while preserving their "blue blood" aristocracy. While it is easy to see the evil in the philosophies of Margaret Sanger, she pales in comparison to others.

Many of the elite feel the military is the face of evil. Sometimes this may be true but for the most part the evil is only the instrument men of evil/power use to fulfill their goals. Evil can easily be seen in the African nation of Somalia*, peacekeepers on a mission were so brazen they actually took pictures of their atrocities, trophy photos, as souvenirs. Soldiers snapped away as they pinned a man to the ground and allegedly shocked his genitals with wires from a radio generator.

Other soldiers took photos as they bound a woman to an armored truck and allegedly raped her with a flare gun. Soldiers also were photographed roasting a boy over an open fire. A witness said the boy went into shock after his clothes caught on fire. The soldiers were acquitted of torture* after the child couldn't be located. The soldiers claimed it was just a game to discourage the boy from stealing.

One soldier also says his commanders had issued orders* to "rough up" the locals and even had the soldiers set out food and water for "bait" to lure hungry Somalis into the shooting range for a "turkey shoot". One witness remembers hearing the troops yell "I got one!"

The soldiers tied up a 16-year-old Somali boy at a weapons bunker*, nicknamed "the pit", who had been hanging around the compound. The soldier says the corporal who was supervising him blindfolded the boy, bound his legs, and tied his hands behind his back. According to the soldier, the corporal kicked the boy then beat him with a baton and a lead pipe. Soldiers later testified the beating continued for hours and more than a dozen different soldiers came by to watch and some even joined in. In all, more than 80 soldiers heard the boy's screams, and no one came to his rescue. One soldier did pull out his camera and take pictures. He says it was his corporal's idea. A medic later found cigarette burns on the teenager's feet and genitals and evidence that he was raped with the soldiers' baton. After hours of torture, the boy finally died.

Mass graves containing hundreds of corpses in Kosovo were discovered and relatives of some of the thousands of Bosnians massacred in Srebrenica demanded the international community reveal what happened to the more than 8,000 men still missing from what had been declared a "UN-protected safe haven." As Serb forces overran the enclave in 1995, lightly armed troops stood by and top officials refused to call in air strikes sought by a military commander. Shortly after officials negotiated for the safety of soldiers in the enclave, Serb forces executed thousands of Bosnians — many of whom had sought safety in the military compound there. Bodies of all the victims have yet to be found. Most of the corpses discovered in mass graves around the area, some with their hands bound behind their backs, have yet to be identified. So far, just 28 bodies were identified in 1999, compared to 15 in 1998 and 5 in 1997, according to Physicians for Human Rights. Some experts say it could be 15 to 20 years for bodies to be exhumed and identified.

A January 11, 1994 telegram from a General*, commander of military force, to his superiors was only one warning of massive slaughter being prepared in Rwanda. From November 1993 to April 1994, there were dozens of other signals, including an early December letter to the General from high-ranking military officers warning of planned massacres; a press release by a bishop declaring that guns were being distributed to civilians; reports by intelligence agents of secret meetings to coordinate attacks on Tutsi, opponents of Hutu Power and other military soldiers and public incitement to murder in the press and on the radio. Foreign observers did not track every indicator, but representatives of several countries were well-informed about most of them. In January, an analyst of U.S. Central Intelligence Agency knew enough to predict that as many as half a million persons might die in case of renewed conflict and, in February, Belgian authorities already feared genocide would occur.

In the early months of 1994, the General repeatedly requested a stronger mandate, more troops and more materiel. Instead of strengthening the mandate and sending reinforcements, the powers that be made only small changes in the rate of troop deployment, measures too limited to affect the development of the situation. When the violence began, the civilian in charge of military forces instructed the military leaders to not become involved. The General was shouting the need for immediate and decisive action. By late April, representatives of other countries sought information beyond that provided by the civilian in charge of troops and became convinced that the slaughter was a genocide that must be stopped. Other countries finally began to intervene to stop the slaughter. Over 500,000 people were exterminated!

It is no secret of another genocide taking place in Darfur. There is now some debate across the government about whether genocide continues, although there is no doubt that extensive murder and other terror are ongoing. Again foreign military troops were present but failed to intervene. This genocide resulted in over 400,000 people losing their lives.

On Dec. 14, 2004, in the predawn hours, a large convoy of foreign troops entered the Port-au-Prince slum of Cite Soleil*. They began firing. A lady was in bed with her 2-year-old son. Her husband got out of bed to get ready for work. The shooting intensified, and she remained in bed beside her child. According to a Harvard Law School report the following occurred:

The lady recalled, "She `felt something warm' on her arm and said to her husband, 'I feel like I got hit with a bullet.' She told us that she realized that 'it wasn't me who had been shot,' as her boy lay limp and lifeless beside her, his 'blood and brain matter were sliding down my arm.' Though she said that she then passed out, her husband told us that a stray bullet had entered their shack with such force that it had removed part of their child's head, leaving him to die in his mother's arms."

When the foreign troops are not engaged in these kinds of incursions, they can usually be found providing support* for the Haitian National Police as they execute peaceful demonstrators demanding the return of their democratically elected president, Jean-Bertrand Aristide. Just last week, five Haitians were killed by the Haitian National Police while foreign troops stood by watching. The Haitians' crime was that they were peacefully

208

demonstrating for the release of political prisoners in Haiti.

The incidents mentioned in the previous paragraphs involving foreign soldiers are a matter of record. There are some who will read this and find it appalling the U.S. Military could do such things. The U.S. Military did not participate in any of these episodes. All these incidents were by U.N Peacekeepers! There are many more reports of atrocities such as gang rapes in the Congo, killings and torture by U.N Peacekeepers around the world. One of the most disturbing incidents that occurred which was mentioned above is the Rwandan genocide. Reportedly, the U.N. military leaders warned of the pending genocide and asked the Security Council be advised for consideration of preventing it. The information was sent to the Under-Secretary-General for Peacekeeping Operations, Kofi Annan! He ordered the peacekeepers to standby and not to take any action. He also failed to present this information to the Security Council until well after the genocide began. Kofi Annan's record as Under-Secretary-General for Peacekeeping Operations is abysmal at best! He failed to provide adequate information and guidance to peacekeepers in Somalia, Bosnia, Sudan and several other African countries.

Kofi Annan became Secretary-General of the United Nations in 1997. Since that time it appears he is on an anti-American crusade and uses every opportunity to attack America's sovereignty and freedoms. He seems to be in lockstep with the likes of Ted Kennedy, John Kerry, Howard Dean and the other anti-American elitists. All ignore the great good this country does, especially for other countries. Take a look at Kofi Annan's accomplishments, statements and hostility toward America.

It has been revealed that between May and June 2003, then U.N. security chief Michael McCann sent his deputy, Bruno Henn (now head of U.N. New York City security), to Baghdad to engage in a "field" survey of the Canal Hotel which had housed U.N. operations prior to the start of Operation Iraqi Freedom in March 2003 and was evacuated when the invasion began. Henn was sent to assess security at the hotel prior to the return of any U.N. personnel. A report on the situation was forwarded to Deputy Secretary-General Louise Frechette, who headed an Annan Iraq action advisory group. Annan has previously denied any direct involvement in such security matters, saying he had left that responsibility to Frechette. Now it has been learned that Annan himself participated in at least two meetings of Frechette's action group prior to the August attack. Henn's security "survey" expressed concern over the situation in Baghdad and raised serious questions about how safe the U.N.

hotel could be made without costly improvements. Frechette, with Annan's approval, opted to "delay" any action on the Henn survey and decided to "vet" the survey with other U.N. departments and seek their "comments" before deciding on what action, if any, should be taken. It was during this period that the U.N. compound was destroyed. It took the secretary-general, who was vacationing in Scandinavia, two days to react. A formal letter of condolence to those who lost friends and relatives was issued almost six months later, only after two investigations had been concluded. It appears the attack might have been averted.

Kofi Annan and the UN have been forging ahead with treaties which ignore the sovereignty of all nations, deny basic human rights and foster socialism. The failure of the Kyoto Protocols in the UN's attempt to control the US, has led to pushing Agenda 21* which is one of the latest propaganda tools being used. The elitists in this country want to mislead you into thinking the signing of this treaty trump the US Constitution. As was shown earlier, this is completely untrue. This global contract attempts to bind governments around the world to the UN plan for changing the ways we live, eat, learn, and communicate - all under the noble banner of saving the earth. Its regulations would severely limit water, electricity, and transportation - even deny human access to our most treasured wilderness areas. If implemented, it would manage and monitor all lands and people. No one would be free from the watchful eye of the new global tracking and information system. As Norman Mailer stated, "The function of socialism is to raise suffering to a higher level."

The elitists have been quietly sliding this concept in "under the radar" by infiltrating local communities with "planners" who manipulate the local politicians into these "sustainable development" plans. If your community has signed off to one of these plans, read it and you will see how it violates many portions of the Bill of Rights and other parts of the Constitution. "Democracy and socialism have nothing in common but one word, equality. But notice the difference: while democracy seeks equality in liberty, socialism seeks equality in restraint and servitude." Alexis de Tocqueville (1805-1859) French statesman & author

This agenda for the 21st Century was originally signed by 178 nations at the UN Conference on Environment and Development in Rio de Janeiro in 1992. Among other things, it called for a Global Biodiversity Assessment of the state of the planet. Prepared by the UN Environmental Programme (UNEP), this GBA armed UN leaders with the "information" and "science" they needed to validate their global management system. Its doomsday predictions were designed to excuse radical population reduction, oppressive lifestyle regulations, and a coercive return to earth-centered religions as the basis for environmental values and self-sustaining human settlements. The GBA concluded on page 763 that "the root causes of the loss of biodiversity are embedded in the way societies use resources." The main culprit, you ask? Judeo-Christian values! Chapter 12.2.3* states that:

This world view is characteristic of large scale societies, heavily dependent on resources brought from considerable distances. It is a world view that is characterized by the denial of sacred attributes in nature, a characteristic that became firmly established about 2000 years ago with the Judeo-Christian-Islamic religious traditions. Eastern cultures with religious traditions such as Buddhism, Jainism and Hinduism did not depart as drastically from the perspective of humans as members of a community of beings including other living and non-living elements.

The apparent goal of the elitists is reduce the greatness of America. Last year a Democrat congressman said we should dismantle our military as we are too powerful and it's not fair to the rest of the world. These foolish thoughts can only come from elitists who believe we should redistribute our wealth to poor countries. What they inevitably fail to realize is we give enormous amount of aid to many underdeveloped countries and the money is stolen by those in power and the people never see it. While in Liberia in 1989, we were given a tour of the medical facilities we were told were built by the UN using American funds. There were several dozen throughout the country. Each was about 30 feet by 60 feet concrete block building, concrete floor and metal roof with open windows and no doors, furniture or equipment. We were told each building cost approximately fifty thousand dollars (about 10 times the actual cost). We see this with the UN on a routine basis. UN officials seek to throw money away apparently to enrich their friends. "The inherent vice of capitalism is the unequal sharing of blessings; the inherent virtue of socialism is the equal sharing of miseries." Winston Churchill (1874-1965)

There are many more facts to show the evil that permeates the United Nations. In my personal experiences with UN representatives I can attest to their arrogance and condescending attitudes. After researching this thoroughly I've come to the conclusion if you have to put one face on the greatest evil which threatens our lives it would have to be Kofi Annan as the face of the United Nations. With the power and influence of the UN, irreparable damage is being spread across the globe. Many of the elitists in this country are in step with the deceptions, lies, distortions and attempts to undermine the freedoms God has bestowed upon us. Perhaps the following is relevant to this situation. "Revelation 17:12 And the ten horns which thou sawest are ten kings, which have received no kingdom as yet; but receive power as kings one hour with the beast. [13] These have one mind, and shall give their power and strength unto the beast."

CHAPTER THIRTEEN

Conclusion

Becoming a police state is not just the abuse by law enforcement (police), but the stranglehold others attempt to place on individuals. When you hear or see someone, especially a local politician or "planner", talk about "protecting the children", "saving the environment" or "for public safety", you can bet whatever follows is a "solution" that imposes restraints, restrictions or outright violates your freedoms. These elitists have been moving closer and closer to socialism throughout America. Since they "feel" they are the intellectually elite or the "enlightened" ones, the agenda they advance doesn't apply to them. Many support the UN's goal of removing private property ownership rights and nationalizing this property. This reflects the failed Former Soviet doctrine. It was John Adams who said: "Property is surely a right of mankind as real as liberty." Mankind has rights, governments do not.

When the elites gain influence one of the first goals is to infringe on our freedoms while exempting themselves from the same restrictions. This socialist mentality is one of the most destructive devices evil uses. History has proven time and again, socialism is the greatest threat to civilization. It promotes laziness, impedes motivation and punishes individuality. The founders of Planned Parenthood and the ACLU are excellent examples of this. Arnold Beichmen, Hoover Institute Fellow states, "...the myth of socialism is far stronger than the reality of capitalism. That is because capitalism is not really an ism at all. It is what people do if you leave them alone." The elitists/socialists can't afford to leave us alone. This is one of the reasons for their anti-American behavior. For over two hundred years the citizens of our country were left alone and we have become the greatest country to ever exist. The elitists/socialists are taking steps to end our greatness!

Look throughout our nation and you will see many different facets of the attempts to infringe on our freedoms and rights God has given us. About 50 years ago the "junk science" of psychology gained significantly more influence in our society. Notice the ills of society began to bloom and flourish about the same time. This also seems to coincide with the departure from spirituality (religion). Put two and two together and you get four unless you're talking to the "progressive" teachers who will accept five for the answer. Up until the elitists push of psychiatry and advent of many psych medications the citizens of this country put their faith and psychological well being into ministers, priests, rabbis and other men of religion. When our society relied on our spiritual needs and problems be vested in our religious leaders we had less problems individually and in society. With the help of the media the spiritual and psychiatric needs were gradually filtered from religion to the secular world of "junk medicine". This is only another attempt to rid God from our everyday lives.

The ACLU has undertaken actions and with the help of activist judges seriously infringes on individual rights. Occasionally the ACLU will fight a just fight, probably to keep up appearances of fighting for the little guy. They attempt to manipulate our legislatures to essentially strip our rights protected under the Bill of Rights. As stated by William Orville Douglas (1898-1980) US Supreme Court associate justice, "When a legislature undertakes to proscribe the exercise of a citizen's constitutional rights it acts lawlessly and the citizen can take matters into his own hands and proceed on the basis that such a law is no law at all." This is what the elites are afraid of. Citizens who know our countries history and know it is we, who have the power and when necessary will take measures to rid our society of evils which threaten our way of life. Look to the Declaration of Independence and you will read our founding fathers were adamant about "we the people" taking charge when necessary. The following is an exert from the Declaration of Independence: "But when a long train of abuses and usurpations, pursuing invariably the same Object evinces a design to reduce them under absolute Despotism, it is their right, it is their duty, to throw off such Government, and to provide new Guards for their future security…"!

We see the infringements more at the local level than federal. Unrealistic zoning, unconstitutional use of eminent domain laws (which the Supreme Court recently used international law to justify) and judicial activism by far left judges who legislate from the bench. The absurdity of the elite is almost comical if it weren't so serious in the restrictions of our lives. I attended a public meeting for a township which was attempting to develop a zoning plan. One of the "planners" brought up the subject of "light pollution". When asked for a definition the "planners" said, "Light pollution is any light which spills over your property boundary. An example is when you turn you porch light on and the light illuminates the public sidewalk and street or neighbor's yard then we have 'light pollution'!" The chief "planner" went on to say provisions should be in the plan to impose a tax on this pollution which will be proportionate to the amount of illumination outside of your property. Just think, if these elitists get their way, you will pay a tax just for turning on you lights even if it's an inside light that happens to reflect out the window onto your neighbor's property.

As stated previously, judicial activism is a one way street. The extreme left have been so adept at loading the judicial system with activist judges we have become numb to some of the outrageous rulings. Yet, the media is quick to pounce on judges who uphold the law and constitution as it is written. Look at the cases of parental notification laws. When a judge upholds the rights of parents, such as Justice Priscilla Owens, the elite media in collusion with organizations like Planned Parenthood and the ACLU attack the decisions and label them as "activists". It's almost amusing!

The entertainment crowd (Hollywood, music, etc…), appear to be the most influential due to their screen persona. This considerable influence can be greatly misused. Many impressionable young people apparently confuse the lines between realities and make believe and some in the entertainment crowd take advantage of this. Talk to a young adult sometime and see how much they know about the world around them. While there are many young adults who are "up to snuff" many are not unless you talk about video games, television or some other computer entertainment. This reminds me of my last assignment in the military. When our computer network went down and was not expected to come back on-line for a few days, all the middle managers (in their 20s and 30s) came to me and said this was a work stoppage and what were we to do? I planned ahead because I envisioned this happening one day. I simply gave each one a pen and paper and said, "This is how we used to do it!" They were insulted because I reduced their workload to the basic principal for getting things done.

Self reliance is one of the most important attributes to ensure our society thrives because it encourages people to think outside the box. The entertainment crowd pushes their ideas, habits, clothing, morals and their way of living on our society. While watching movies, television, listening to music and reading can be good entertainment we have to be alert to the subtle messages in the content. This affects your subconscious mind without you even noticing it. This is why you are seeing more name brand items in many of these shows you watch frequently. What better advertisement than to discreetly slide a soda can or chips for name recognition into a program? It also happens with the liberal messages.

The far left along with the elite media has had almost free reign for over

40 years. It's no wonder our values have been distorted and manipulated in their unfettered attempt to destroy everything the United Stated stands for. I remember sometime around 2000/2001 of watching a news program that had a panel of several guests evenly split between liberal and conservative. When asked about the liberal bias in the media, the conservative said with the advent of cable news and proliferation of talk radio the conservatives now can get their message out. The liberal guest (I believe he was part of Al Gore's campaign) shifted in his chair and responded by saying, "it's not fair the right now has a voice." When challenged about the liberal bias he said the right didn't deserve this much time and the left didn't have the media outlets the right has. When it was pointed out NBC, CBS, CNN, New York Times, Washington Post and many others were left leaning media outlets he essentially said, "So what!" This is typical of the elite crowd. Now the right is getting equal time the left is getting desperate. I believe this is why the left is going all out now. The average American is now getting both sides and the elite media's force feeding the liberal agenda is becoming more evident and hardworking Americans don't want it.

The elite want to continue the handouts not only in our country but to other countries as well. This quote by

Theodore Roosevelt contradicts these socialists, "The first requisite of a good citizen in this Republic of ours is that he shall be able and willing to pull his weight."

The elitists know we can not be conquered as long as we refuse to let our freedoms die. Noah Webster (1758-1843) provides the best argument to preserve our Bill of Rights, "Before a standing army can rule, the people must be disarmed; as they are in almost every kingdom in Europe. The supreme power in America cannot enforce unjust laws by the sword; because the whole body of the people are armed, and constitute a force superior to any band of regular troops that can be, on any pretence, raised in the United States. A military force, at the command of Congress, can execute no laws, but such as the people perceive to be just and constitutional; for they will possess the power and jealousy will instantly inspire the inclination, to resist the execution of a law which appears to them unjust and oppressive."

If you are one of these elitists, this is to put you on notice! The average person in America works hard is spiritual and has had enough! Close to 90 percent of Americans do not like the direction you elitists are taking our country. We have not only the right but the responsibility to take corrective action even if it means the destruction of

political and judicial lives! We must
ensure the US Constitution will prevail
so we can proudly boast our allegiance to
"Freedom, Family, Country and God!"

END NOTES

Sources and Support

CHAPTER ONE
Rewriting History
by Dick Morris (Hardcover - May 1, 2004)

Soviet Union (Former) — Constitution
Adopted on: 7 Oct 1977 }
{ICL Document Status: 7 Oct 1977 }

Rosie O'Donnell Show
May 19, 1999

Michael Moore's Bodyguard Arrested on Airport Gun Charge Thursday, New York January 20, 2005

AMERICA'S 1ST FREEDOM
Official Journal of the National Rifle Association
The Latest From www.NRALive.com, page 20
June, 2000

CHAPTER TWO
Why a Mom's Fate Should Worry Us All
By SANDY BANKS, Los Angeles Times
April 27, 2001

Atwater v. Lago Vista, 99-1408.
By ANNE GEARAN, Associated Press Writer

A World Without Guns
By Dave Kopel, Paul Gallant, and Joanne Eisen of the Independence Institute December 5, 2001 9:40 a.m.

Trend: You smoke? You're fired! Posted By Stephanie Armour, USA TODAY 5/11/2005 11:43 PM

CHAPTER THREE
MEDIA VIOLENCE LINKED TO "CULTURE OF DISRESPECT"
Polk County Gail Peavey, Family Living Agent
Focus on Family Living August 5, 2004

American Education and Indoctrination Are Synonymous By George M. Haddad, January 26, 2005
http://www.webcommentary.com/asp/ShowArticle.asp?id=had dadg&date=050124

State Senate bill's language on teaching history worries educators.
West Palm Beach Post, 24 April 2005

Police Handcuff, Arrest 5-Year-Old Girl
By THOMAS C. TOBIN, Times Staff Writer
PETERSBURG TIMES, April 22, 2005ST.

Devil Worship. A Growing Menace In The 90's
by Don Humphrey, published in Church Growth (January - March, 1990): 5 - 6.

U.S. Teenage Pregnancy Statistics
Overall Trends, Trends by Race and Ethnicity
The Alan Guttmacher Institute
120 Wall Street, New York, NY 10005
www.guttmacher.org Updated February 19, 2004

Lexington school calls cops on dad irate over gay book,
By Laura Crimaldi Thursday, April 28, 2005
Boston Herald.com

CHAPTER FOUR

Measure 37
Proposed by initiative petition voted on at the General Election, November 2, 2004.

A Path to the Future
Shelby County Comprehensive Master Plan
ZONING REGULATIONS of SHELBY COUNTY, ALABAMA
Including revisions through: - May 4, 2004 —

KPS Group, Inc., Birmingham, Alabama Departments
Member Profile July 1999

Soros's Deep Pockets vs. Bush
By Laura Blumenfeld Washington Post Staff Writer
Tuesday, November 11, 2003; Page A03

American Planning Association
http://www.planning.org/

CHAPTER FIVE

Modern IQ ranges for various occupations
http://members.shaw.ca/delajara/Occupations.html

Conspiracy theories on Ohio vote refuse to die
Bill Lubinger Plain Dealer Reporter Sunday, December 05, 2004

Breaking New Ground
by Linda Hussa Western Horseman Magazine March 2005

Fox News Channel

Your World with Neil Cavuto February 22, 2005

Liberty and law 2004
The Norwood, Ohio Eminent Domain Trial:
By Scott Bullock
http://www.ij.org/staff/bullock.html

ABA HISTORY
Founded on August 21,1878
http://www.abanet.org/

Founding of AMA at Academy of Natural Sciences in Philadelphia, 1847: (Founder, Nathan S. Davis MD)
http://www.ama-assn.org/

Soviet Union (Former) — Constitution
Adopted on: 7 Oct 1977 }
{ICL Document Status: 7 Oct 1977}

CHAPTER SIX
DOD Active Duty Military Personnel Strength Levels, Fiscal Years 1950-2002

CIVILIAN EMPLOYMENT STATISTICS
September 2004

DOD DIRECT HIRE CIVILIAN PERSONNEL STRENGTH - COMPONENT DETAIL FISCAL YEARS 1977 — 2001

DOD DIRECT HIRE CIVILIAN PERSONNEL STRENGTH LEVELS FISCAL YEARS 1950 — 2001

CHAPTER SEVEN
DA: Police failures in Sheridan case 'critical'
By ED ZAGORSKI - GM Today Staff   October 11, 2004

Clinton Regime Outdoes Itself by Snatching Elian Gonzalez, by Deroy Murdock April 24, 2000 CATO Institute

Video: As family shrieks, police kill dog
COOKEVILLE, Tennessee (CNN)
Wednesday, January 8, 2003 Posted: 10:26 PM EST

CHAPTER EIGHT
Smallest baby ever close to leaving Illinois hospital,
The Associated Press
Updated: 6:40 p.m. ET Dec. 21, 2004

Smallest Baby to Survive in New Jersey — Second Smallest in the Nation — Born at Saint Barnabas Medical Center NICU, 2003

Legal Status
By Thomas R. Lenz, DVM., MS American Quarter Horse
Journal February 2005, page 10

Task force on legal status of animals approved
EXECUTIVE BOARD COVERAGE, July 15, 2004
http://www.avma.org/

The Rabies Vaccination and Verification Program
Shelby County, Alabama effective January 1, 2005.

CHAPTER NINE
Atwater v. Lago Vista, 99-1408.
By ANNE GEARAN, Associated Press Writer

David Smith, Let Russell Yates Grieve
MOORE, South Carolina (CNN) July 6, 2001 Posted: 10:56
AM EDT (1456 GMT)

Supreme Court Rules Cities May Seize Homes
By HOPE YEN, AP Updated: 05:22 PM EDT

Impeach O'Connor And Breyer!
By Tom Barrett November 6, 2003
http://www.americandaily.com/article/1594

So Much for the Consent of the Governed
By Frank Salvato February 18, 2005
http://www.mensnewsdaily.com/archive/s/salvato/2005/sal
vato021805.htm

CHAPTER TEN
**The United Nations Conference on Human Settlements
(Habitat I),** Vancouver, May 31 - June 11, 1976. Agenda
Item 10 of the Conference Report

U.N. influence in Alabama
By Henry Lamb 2003 WorldNetDaily.com Posted: May 24,
2003 1:00 a.m. Eastern

The Incredible Shrinking AIDS Epidemic
By Michael Fumento The American Spectator, May 1989 by
The American Spectator

The Shodor Education Foundation, Inc.
in cooperation with the
North Carolina State University
Cooperative Extension Service
Neuse River Education Team

Earth's Oceans Had A Simple Source
Dr. Thomas Gold
http://xenotechresearch.com/moceans.htm

The Exxon Valdez Oil Spill
Office of Response and Restoration, National Ocean
Service, National Oceanic and Atmospheric
Administration Revised: May 28, 2003

**Ecoterrorism: Extremism in the Animal Rights and
Environmentalist Movements**
Anti-Defamation League (ADL) Law Enforcement Agency
Resource Network 2004 Report

Environmentalism, Eco-Terrorism and Endangered Species
by Glenn Woiceshyn   (January 25, 1999)
http://capmag.com/article.asp?ID=217

KYOTO PROTOCOL
The United Nations Framework Convention on Climate
Change, adopted in New York on 9 May 1992.

**"COSPEC" helps observatory scientists study volcanic
pollution and processes** June 25, 1998
http://hvo.wr.usgs.gov/volcanowatch/98_06_25.html

Ocean Water: Salinity
http://www.onr.navy.mil/focus

Guess what? Antarctica's getting colder, not warmer
By Peter N. Spotts | Staff writer of The Christian
Science Monitor News Service February 14, 2002

CHAPTER ELEVEN
Omega Letter Christian Intelligence Digest
America's Communist Lawyers' Union
Omega Letter Editor, Prophecy — Signs, Thursday,
December 02, 2004

**Sexual Disorientation: Faulty Research In The
Homosexual Debate**
Family Research Council paper by Robert Knight
www.epm.org

The Incredible Shrinking AIDS Epidemic
By Michael Fumento The American Spectator, May 1989 by
The American Spectator

CHAPTER TWELVE
"Killer Angel"
By George Grant, Reformer Press,

The Pivot of Civilization
by Margaret Sanger (founder of Planned Parenthood)

Woman's Body, Woman's Right,
By Linda Gordon, New York: Penguin Press

Disturbing the peace
Dateline' uncovers violence committed by U.N.
peacekeepers January 2005

Soldiers who held boy over fire go free
By Robert Fox, International News Tuesday 1 July 1997
Electronic Telegraph Issue 767

**Darfur Destroyed: Ethnic Cleansing by Government and
Militia Forces in Western Sudan,** Human Rights Watch
Report, May 7, 2004

Darfur in Flames: Atrocities in Western Sudan
Human Rights Watch Report, April 2, 2004

Diplomacy By Death Squad
By IRA KURZBAN 05/03/05 "Counterpunch.org"

Local Agenda 21
The U.N. Plan for Your Community
By Berit Kjos — 1998
http://www.crossroad.to/text/articles/la21_198.html

**Agenda 21, the Rio Declaration on Environment and
Development, and the Statement of principles for the
Sustainable Management of Forests**
United Nations Conference on Environment and
Development (UNCED) Rio de Janerio, Brazil, 3 to 14
June 1992

Manufactured by Amazon.ca
Bolton, ON